Take tin̲_____is month to
kick bac_____lequin Presents
novel. We hope you enjoy this month's selection.

If you love royal heroes, you're in for a treat this month!
In Penny Jordan's latest book, *The Italian Duke's Wife*,
an Italian aristocrat chooses a young English woman
as his convenient wife. When he unleashes within
her a desire she never knew she possessed, he is soon
regretting his no-consummation rule.... Emma Darcy's
sheikh in *Traded to the Sheikh* is an equally powerful
and sexy alpha male. This story has a wonderfully exotic
desert setting, too!

We have some gorgeous European men this month.
*Shackled by Diamonds* by Julia James is part of our
popular miniseries GREEK TYCOONS. Read about a
Greek tycoon and the revenge he plans to exact on an
innocent, beautiful model when he wrongly suspects
her of stealing his priceless diamonds. In Sarah Morgan's
*Public Wife, Private Mistress*, can a passionate Italian's
marriage be rekindled when he is unexpectedly reunited
with his estranged wife?

In *The Antonides Marriage Deal* by Anne McAllister, a
Greek magnate meets a stunning new business partner,
and he begins to wonder if he can turn their business
arrangement into a permanent contract—such as
marriage! Kay Thorpe's *Bought by a Billionaire* tells of
a Portuguese billionaire and his ex-lover. He wants her
back as his mistress. Previously she rejected his proposal
because of his arrogance and his powerful sexuality. But
this time he wants marriage....

Happy reading! Look out for a brand-new selection next
month.

*Legally wed,
but he's never said
"I love you!"
They're...
Wedlocked!*

**The series where marriages are made
in haste...and love comes later....**

*Look out for more WEDLOCKED!
wedding stories available only from
Harlequin Presents®.*

# Anne McAllister

# THE ANTONIDES MARRIAGE DEAL

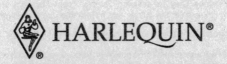

# HARLEQUIN®

TORONTO • NEW YORK • LONDON
AMSTERDAM • PARIS • SYDNEY • HAMBURG
STOCKHOLM • ATHENS • TOKYO • MILAN • MADRID
PRAGUE • WARSAW • BUDAPEST • AUCKLAND

ISBN 0-373-12533-X

THE ANTONIDES MARRIAGE DEAL

First North American Publication 2006.

## All about the author…
*Anne McAllister*

RITA® Award winner **ANNE MCALLISTER** was born
in California. She spent formative summer vacations on
the beach near her home, on her grandparents' small
ranch in Colorado and visiting relatives in Montana.
Studying the cowboys, the surfers and the beach
volleyball players, she spent long hours developing her
concept of "the perfect hero." (Have you noticed a lack
of hard-driving type A businessmen among them? Well,
she promises to do one soon, just for a change!)

One thing she did do, early on, was develop a weakness
for lean, dark-haired, handsome lone-wolf type of guys.
When she finally found one, he was in the university
library where she was working. She knew a good
man when she saw one. They've now been sharing
"happily ever afters" for over thirty years. They have
four grown children, and a steadily increasing number
of grandchildren. They also have three dogs, who keep
her fit by taking her on long walks every day.

Quite a few years ago they moved to the Midwest, but
they spend more and more time in Montana. And as
Anne says, she lives there in her head most of the time
anyway. She wishes a small town like her very own
Elmer, Montana, existed. She'd move there in a minute.
But she loves visiting big cities as well, and New York
has always been her favorite.

Before she started writing romances, Anne taught
Spanish, capped deodorant bottles copyedited
textbooks, got a master's degree in theology and
ghostwrote sermons. Strange and varied, perhaps, but
all grist for the writer's mill, she says.

For Aunt Billie
with love forever

# CHAPTER ONE

"YOUR father is on line six."

Elias Antonides stared at the row of red lights blinking on his desk phone and thanked God he'd declined the ten-line option he'd been offered when he'd begun renovating and converting the riverside warehouse into the new Brooklyn-based home of Antonides Marine International nine months ago.

"Right," he said. "Thanks, Rosie. Put him on hold."

"He says it's important," his assistant informed him.

"If it's important, he'll wait," Elias said, reasonably confident that he wouldn't do anything of the sort.

Aeolus Antonides had the staying power of a fruit fly. Named for the god of the wind, according to him, and "the god of hot air," in Elias's view, Aeolus was as charming and feckless a man as had ever lived. As president of Antonides Marine, he enjoyed three-hour lunches and three olive martinis, playing golf with his cronies and taking them out in his sailboat, but he had no patience for day-to-day routine, for turning red ink into black, for anything that resembled a daily grind. He didn't want to know that they would benefit from some ready cash or that Elias was contemplating the purchase of a small marine outfitter that would expand their holdings. Business bored him. Talking to his son bored him.

And chances were excellent today that, by the time Elias had dealt with the other five blinking lights, his father would have hung up and gone off to play another round of golf or out for a sail from his Hamptons home.

In fact, Elias was counting on it. He loved his father dearly, but he didn't need the old man meddling in business matters. Whatever his father wanted, it would invariably complicate his life.

And he had enough complications already today—though it wasn't much different from any other.

His sister Cristina, on line two, wanted him to help her set up the financing for a bead store.

"A *bead* store?" Elias thought he'd heard everything. Cristina had variously wanted to raise rabbits, tie-dye T-shirts and go to disk-jockey school. But the beads were new.

"So I can stay in New York," she explained perfectly reasonably. "Mark's in New York."

Mark was her latest boyfriend. Elias didn't think he'd be her last. Famous for racing speedboats and chasing women, Mark Batakis was as likely to be here today and gone tomorrow as Cristina's bead-store aspirations.

"No, Cristina," he said firmly.

"But—"

"No. You come up with a good business plan for something and we'll talk. Until then, no." And he hung up before she could reply.

His mother, on line three, was arranging a dinner party on the weekend. "Are you bringing a girlfriend?" she asked hopefully. "Or shall I arrange one."

Elias gritted his teeth. "I don't need you arranging dates for me, Mother," he said evenly, knowing full well as he did so that his words fell on deaf ears.

Helena Antonides's goal in life was to see him married and providing her with grandchildren. Inasmuch as he'd been married once disastrously and had no intention of ever being married again, Elias could have told her she was doomed to fail. She had other children, let them have the grandchildren she was so desperate for.

Besides, wasn't it enough that he was providing the financial support for the entire Antonides clan to live in the manner to which three generations of them had become accustomed? Apparently not.

"Well—" she sniffed, annoyed at him as usual "—you don't seem to be doing a very good job yourself."

"Thank you for sharing your opinion," Elias said politely.

He never bluntly told his mother that he was not ever getting married again, because she would have argued with him, and as far as Elias was concerned, the matter wasn't up for debate. He had been divorced for seven years, had purposely made no effort at all to find anyone to replace the duplicitous, avaricious Millicent, and had no intention of doing so.

Surely after seven years his mother should have noticed that.

"Don't go all stuffy on me, Elias Antonides. I've got your best interests at heart. You should be grateful."

As that didn't call for an answer, Elias didn't supply one. "I have to go, Mom, I have work to do."

"You always have work to do."

"Someone has to."

There was a dead silence on the other end of the line. She couldn't deny it, but she wouldn't agree, either. At last Helena said firmly, "Just be here Sunday. I'll provide the girl." She was the one who hung up on him.

His sister, Martha, on line four, was brimming with ideas for her painting. Martha always had ideas—and rarely had the means to see them through.

"If you want me to do a good job on those murals," she told him, "I really should go back to Greece."

"What for?"

"Inspiration," she said cheerfully.

"A vacation, you mean." Elias knew his sister. Martha was a good artist. He wouldn't have asked her to cover the wall of the foyer of his building, not to mention one in his office and the other in his bedroom if she were a hack. But he didn't feel like subsidizing her summer holidays, either. "Forget it. I'll send you some photos. You can work from them."

Martha sighed. "You're such a killjoy, Elias."

"Everyone knows that," he agreed. "Deal with it."

On line five Martha's twin, Lukas, didn't want to deal with it. "What's wrong with going to New Zealand?" Lukas wanted to know.

"Nothing's wrong with it," Elias said with more patience than he felt. "But I thought you were going to Greece?"

"I did. I'm in Greece," Lukas informed him. "But it's boring here. There's nothing to do. I met some guys at the taverna last night. They're heading to New Zealand. I thought I'd go, too. So do you know someone there—in Auckland, say—who might want to hire me for a while?"

"To do what?" It was a fair question. Lukas had graduated from college with a major in ancient languages. None of them was Maori.

"Doesn't matter. Whatever," Lukas said vaguely. "Or I could go to Australia. Maybe go walkabout?"

Which seemed to be pretty much what he was already doing, Elias thought, save for the fact that he wasn't confining his wandering to Australia as their brother Peter had.

"You could come home and go to work for me," Elias suggested not for the first time.

"No way," Lukas said not for the first time, either. "I'll give you a call when I get to Auckland to see if you have any ideas."

Ted Corbett—on line one—the only legitimate caller as far as Elias was concerned, was fortunately still there.

"So, what do you think? Ready to take us over?" That was why he was still there. Corbett was eager to sell his marine outfitters business and just as eager for Elias to be the one to buy it.

"We're thinking about it," Elias said. "No decision yet. Paul has been doing some research, running the numbers."

His projects manager loved ferreting out all the details that went into these decisions. Elias, who didn't, left Paul to it. But ultimately Elias was going to have to make the final decision. All the decisions, in the end, were his.

"I want to come out and see the operation in person," he said.

"Of course," Corbett agreed. "Whenever you want." He chattered on about the selling points, and Elias listened.

He deliberately took his time with Corbett, eyeing the red light on line six all the while. It stayed bright red. When he finally finished with Corbett it was still blinking. Probably the old man just walked off and left his phone on. That would be just like him. But Elias punched the button anyway.

"My, you're a busy fellow," Aeolus boomed in his ear.

Elias shut his eyes and mustered his patience. His father must have been doing the crossword to wait so long. "Actually, yes. I've been on the phone way too long, and now I'm late for a meeting. What's up?"

"Me, actually. Came into the city to see a friend. Thought I'd stop by. Got something to discuss with you."

The last thing Elias needed today was his father making a personal appearance. "I'm coming out on the weekend," Elias said, hoping to forestall the visit. "We can talk then."

But Aeolus was otherwise inclined. "This won't take long. See you in a bit." And the phone clicked in Elias's ear.

Damn it! How typical of his father. It didn't matter how busy you were, if he wanted your attention, Aeolus found a way to get it. Elias banged the phone down and pinched the bridge of his nose, feeling a headache gathering force back behind his eyes.

By the time his beaming father breezed straight past Rosie and into Elias's office an hour later, Elias's headache was raging full-bore.

"Guess what I did!" Aeolus kicked the door shut and did one of the little soft-shuffle steps that invariably followed his sinking a particularly tricky putt.

"Hit a hole in one?" Elias guessed. He stood up so he could meet his father head-on.

At the golf reference, Aeolus's smile grew almost wistful. "I wish," he murmured. He sighed, then brightened. "But, metaphorically speaking, I guess you could say that."

Metaphorically speaking? Since when did Aeolus Antonides speak in metaphors? Elias raised his eyebrows and waited politely for his father's news.

Aeolus rubbed his hands together and beamed. "I found us a business partner!"

"*What!*" Elias stared at his father, appalled. "What the hell do you mean, business partner? We don't need a business partner!"

"You said we needed ready cash."

Oh, hell. He *had* been listening. "I never said anything about a business partner! The business is doing fine!"

"Of course it is," Aeolus nodded. "Couldn't get a partner if it weren't. No rats want to board sinking ships."

Rats? Elias felt the hair on the back of his neck stand up. "What rats?"

"Nothing. No rats," Aeolus said quickly. "Just a figure of speech."

"Well, forget it."

"No. You work too hard, Elias. I know I haven't done my part. It's just…it's not in me. I—" Aeolus looked bleak.

"I know that, Dad." Elias gave his father a sincere, sympathetic smile. "I understand." Which was the truth. "Don't worry about it. It's not a problem."

Not now at least. Eight years ago it had cost him his marriage.

No, that wasn't fair. His father's lack of business acumen had been only one factor in the breakup with Millicent. It had begun when he'd toyed with quitting business school to start his own boat-building company, to do what his grandfather had done. Millicent had been appalled. She'd been passionate about him finishing school and stepping in at Antonides. But that was when she'd thought it was worth something. When she found out its books were redder than a sunset, she'd been appalled, and livid when Elias had insisted on staying and trying to salvage the firm.

No, his father's business incompetence had only highlighted the problems between himself and Millicent. The truth was that he should have realized what Millicent's priorities were and never married her in the first place. It was a case of extraordinary bad judgement and one Elias was not going to repeat.

"But I do worry," his father went on. "We both do, your mother and I. You work so hard. Too hard."

Elias had never spoken of the reasons for the divorce, but his parents weren't fools. They knew Elias had worked almost 24/7 to salvage the business from the state it had slid to due to his father's not-so-benign neglect. They knew that the financial reality of Antonides Marine did not meet the expectations of their son's social-ladder climbing wife. They knew she had vanished not long after Elias dropped out of business school to work in the family firm. And within weeks of the divorce being final, Millicent had married the heir to a Napa Valley winery.

Of course no one mentioned any of this. For years no one had spoken her name, least of all Elias.

But shortly after Millicent's marriage, the fretting began—and so had the parade of eligible women, as if getting Elias a new wife would make things better, make his father feel less guilty.

As far as Elias was concerned, his father had no need to feel guilty. Aeolus was who he was. Millicent was who she was. And Elias was who he was—a man who didn't want a wife.

Or a business partner.

"No, Dad," he said firmly now.

Aeolus shrugged. "Sorry. Too late. It's done. I sold forty percent of Antonides Marine."

Elias felt as if he'd been punched. "*Sold it?* You can't do that!"

Aeolus's whole demeanor changed in an instant. He was no longer the amiable, charming father Elias knew and loved. Drawing himself up sharply with almost military rigidity, he looked down his not inconsiderable nose at his furious son.

"Of course I can sell it," Aeolus said stiffly, his tone infused with generations of Greek arrogance that even his customary amiable temperament couldn't erase. "I own it."

"Yes, I know that. But—" But it was true. Aeolus did own Antonides Marine. Or fifty percent of it anyway. Elias owned ten percent. Forty percent was in trust for his four siblings. It was a

family company. Always had been. No one whose name was not
Antonides had ever owned any of it.

Elias stared at his father, feeling poleaxed. Gutted. Betrayed.
He swallowed. "Sold it?" he echoed hollowly. Which meant
what? That his work of the past eight years was, like his marriage, gone in the stroke of a pen?

"Not all of it," Aeolus assured him. "Just enough to give you
a little capital. You said you needed money. All last Sunday at
your mother's dinner party you were on the phone talking to
someone about raising capital to buy some outfitter."

"And I was doing it." Elias ground out.

"Well, now I've done it instead." His father rubbed his hands
together briskly. "So you don't have to work so hard. You have
breathing room."

*"Breathing room?"* Elias would have laughed if he hadn't already been gasping. His knees felt weak. He wanted to sit down.
He wanted to put his head between his knees and take deep desperate breaths. But instead he stood rigid, his fingers balled into
fists, and stared at his father in impotent fury, none of which he
allowed to show on his face.

"You didn't need to sell," he said at last in measured tones that
he congratulated himself did not betray the rage he felt. "It would
have been all right."

"Oh, yes? Then why did we move here?" Aeolus wrinkled his
nose as he looked around the newly renovated offices in the riverside warehouse Elias had bought and which until today his father had never seen.

"To get back to our roots," Elias said through his teeth. There
was no reason at all to pay midtown Manhattan prices when his
business could be better conducted from Brooklyn. "This is
where *Papu* had his first offices." His grandfather had never
wanted to be far from water.

Aeolus didn't seem convinced. "Well, it's obvious that things
aren't what they used to be," he said with a look around. "I
wanted to help."

Help? Dear God! Elias took a wild, shuddering breath, raked

a hand through his hair. With help like this he might as well throw in the towel.

Of course, he wouldn't.

Antonides Marine was his life. Since he'd shelved his dream of building his own boats, since Millicent had walked out, it was the only thing he'd focused on. She would have said, of course, that it was the only thing he'd focused on *before* she'd left him. But that wasn't true. And he'd done it in the first place for her, to try to give her the life she'd wanted. How was he to know she'd just been looking for an excuse to walk out?

Now it was all he had. All he lived for. He was determined to restore it to the glory his great-grandfather and his grandfather had achieved. And he was almost there.

But it hadn't been an easy road so far, and he shouldn't expect it would start now. Deliberately he straightened his tie and pasted a smile on his face and told himself it would be all right.

This was just one more bump in the road. There had been plenty of bumps—and potholes—and potential disasters in the road since he'd taken over running Antonides Marine.

With luck he could even work out a deal to buy the shares Aeolus had sold away. Yes. That was a good idea. Then there would be no more opportunity for his father to do something foolish behind his back.

Elias flexed his shoulders, worked to ease the tension in them, took another, calmer breath and then turned to his father, prepared to make the best of it.

"Sold it to whom?" he asked politely.

"Socrates Savas."

"The hell you say!"

So much for calm. So much for polite. So much for making the best of it!

"Socrates Savas is a pirate. A scavenger! He buys up failing companies, guts them, then sells off what's left for scrap!" Elias was yelling. He knew he was yelling. He couldn't help it.

"He does have a certain reputation," Aeolus admitted, the characteristic smile not in evidence now.

"An entirely deserved reputation," Elias snarled. He stalked around the room. He wanted to punch the walls. Wanted to punch his father. "Damn it to hell! Antonides Marine is *not* failing!"

"So I hear. Socrates said it was doing very well indeed. He had to give me a pile for it," Aeolus reflected with considerable satisfaction. "So much that he complained about it. Said he should have bought it five years ago. Said it was too bad he hadn't known about it then."

Which had been the whole point. One look at the Antonides Marine's books eight years ago, and Elias had known their days as a company were numbered unless he could drag them back into the black.

He'd done it. But it had meant long long hours and cost-cutting and streamlining and reorganization and doing all of it without allowing the company to look as if it were in any trouble at all. He'd spent years trying to stay under Socrates Savas's radar. For all the good it had done him.

"Good thing for us Socrates didn't notice it then," Aeolus reflected, as if it had just occurred to him.

"Good thing," Elias agreed sarcastically, for once taking no pains to spare his father's feelings.

Aeolus looked momentarily chagrined, but then brightened again and looked at his son approvingly. "You should be proud. You pulled us out of the abyss, Socrates says. Though I don't know as I'd have called it an abyss," he reflected.

"I would've," Elias muttered.

Obviously Savas had had his eye on the business for a while whether Elias had known it or not. Circling like a vulture, no doubt. Not that he'd ever given any indication. But he was a past master at spotting prey, waiting for the right moment, then snapping up a floundering company.

For the past year Elias had dared to breathe easier knowing that Antonides Marine wasn't floundering anymore. And now his father had *sold* the blackguard forty percent of it anyway?

Damnation!

So what did Savas intend to do with it? The possibilities sent chills down Elias's spine. He wouldn't let himself imagine. And he certainly wouldn't hang around to watch. Knowing he couldn't bear it gave him the resolve to say words he never ever thought he'd say.

"Fine," he said, looking his father in the eye. "He can have it. I quit."

His father gaped at him, his normally rosy countenance going suddenly, starkly white. "Quit? *Quit?* But…but, Elias…you *can't* quit!"

"Of course I can." Elias had been blessed with his own share of the Antonides arrogance and hauteur, and if Aeolus could sell the business that his son had rescued from the scrap pile without so much as a nod in his direction, then by God, Elias could certainly quit without looking back!

"But…" Aeolus shook his head helplessly, his hands waving in futility. "You can't." His words were almost a whisper, his face still ashen. There was a pleading note in his voice.

Elias frowned. He had expected *sturm und drang,* not a death mask.

"Why can't I?" he asked with studied politeness, a hint of a not very pleasant smile on his lips.

"Because—" Aeolus's hands fluttered "—because it's…it's written in the contract that you'll stay on."

"You can't sell me with the company, Dad. That's slavery. There're laws against it. So, I guess the contract is null and void?" Elias smiled a real smile now. "All's well that ends well," he added, managing—barely—to restrain himself from rubbing his hands together.

But Aeolus didn't look pleased and his color hadn't returned. His fingers knotted and twisted. His gaze dropped. He didn't look at his son. He looked at the floor without a word.

"What is it?" Elias said warily in the silence.

Still nothing. Not for a long, long time. Then, at last, his father lifted his head. "We'll lose the house."

Elias scowled. "What do you mean, you'll lose the house? What house? The house on Long Island?"

His father gave an almost imperceptible negative shake of his head.

No? *Not* the Long Island house?

Then that meant…

"*Our* house?"

The family home on Santorini? The one his great-grand-father, also called Elias, had built with his bare hands? The one each succeeding generation of Antonides men and women had added to, so that it was home to not only their bodies but their history, their memories, their accomplishments?

Of course, they'd had the house on Long Island for years. They'd had flats in London, in Sydney and in Hong Kong.

But they only had one home.

But his father couldn't mean that. The house on Santorini had nothing to do with the business! Never had. It belonged to his father now as it had belonged to his father and his father's father before him. For four generations the house had gone from eldest son to eldest son.

It would be Elias's someday. And, though he'd saved the company and all its holdings, none of them mattered to him as much as that single house. It held memories of his childhood, of summer days spent working building boats with his grandfather, of the dreams of youth that were pure and untarnished, though life was anything but. The house on Santorini was their strength, their refuge—the physical heart of the Antonides family.

It was the only *thing* Elias loved.

His fingers curled into fists. It was the only way he could keep from grabbing his father by the front of his emerald-green polo shirt and shaking him. *"What have you done to our house?"*

"Nothing," Aeolus said quickly. "Well, nothing if you stay on at Antonides." He shot Elias a quick, hopeful glance that skittered away at once in the face of his son's burning black fury. He wrung his hands. "It was just a small bet. A sailboat race. A bet I made with Socrates. Which boat—his or mine—could sail to Montauk and back faster. I'm a better sailor than Socrates Savas!"

Which Elias had no doubt was true. "So what happened?"

"The bet was about the boats," his father said heavily.

"I know. You raced the boats. So?"

Aeolus shot him an exasperated look. "I'm a better sailor than *Socrates* Savas. I don't hold a candle to his son Theo!"

Elias whistled. "Theo Savas is Socrates's son?"

Even Elias had heard of Theo Savas. Anyone who knew anything about sailing knew Theo Savas. He had sailed for Greece in the Olympics. He had crewed in several America's Cup races. He had done windsurfing and solo sailing voyages that caught the hearts and minds of armchair adventurers everywhere. He was also lean, muscular and handsome, a playboy without equal and, naturally—according to Elias's sisters—the ideal of Greek manhood.

No matter that he had been raised in Queens.

"Theo won," Aeolus said, filling his cheeks with air, then exhaling sharply and shaking his head. "And he gets clear title to the house—unless you agree to stay on as managing director of Antonides Marine for two years."

*"Two years!"*

"It's not much!" Aeolus protested. "Hardly a life sentence."

It might as well be. Elias couldn't believe it. His father was asking him to simply sit here and watch as Socrates Savas gutted the company he had worked so hard to save!

"What the hell did I ever do to him?" Elias demanded.

"Do to him? Why, nothing at all. What do you mean?"

"Nothing. Never mind." There was no reason to take it personally. Socrates Savas did this sort of thing all the time. Still Elias ground his teeth. He felt the pulse pound in his temple and deliberately unclenched his jaw and took a deep, calculated breath.

Two years. It was a price he could pay. He'd paid far bigger ones. And this wasn't just about his life, it was the life of his whole family.

He'd done everything else. How could he not do this?

"All right," he said at last. "I'll stay."

His father beamed, breathed again, pounded him on the back. "I knew you would!"

"But I'm not answering to Socrates Savas. He's *not* running things!"

"Of course not!" His father said, relieved beyond belief. "His daughter is!"

The new president of Antonides Marine International hadn't slept a wink all night.

Tallie had lain awake, grinning ear to ear, her mind whirling with glorious possibilities and the satisfaction of knowing that her father was finally acknowledging she was good at what she did.

She knew it wasn't easy for him. Socrates Savas was as traditional as a stubborn, opinionated Greek father could be—even though he was two generations removed from the old country.

In her father's mind, his four sons were the ones who were supposed to follow his footsteps into the family business. His only daughter, Thalia, ought to stay at home, mend clothes and cook meals and eventually marry a nice, hardworking Greek man and have lots of lovely little dark-haired, dark-eyed Greek grandchildren for Socrates to dandle on his knee.

It wasn't going to happen.

Oh, she would have married. If Lieutenant Brian O'Malley's plane had not crashed seven years ago, she certainly would have married him. Life would have been a lot different.

But since Brian's death she'd never met anyone who'd even tempted her. And not for her father's lack of trying. Sometimes she thought he'd introduced her to every eligible Greek on the East Coast.

"Go pester the boys," she told him. "Go find them wives."

But Socrates just muttered and grumbled about his four sons. They were even more of a mystery to him than Tallie was. If she desperately wanted to follow him into business, Theo, George, Demetrios and Yiannis, had absolutely no interest in their father's footsteps—or his business—at all.

Theo, the eldest, was a world-class open-ocean sailor. Tie him to an office or even stick him in a city and he would die. Socrates wasn't sympathetic. He considered that his oldest son just "mucked about in boats."

George was a brilliant physicist. He was unraveling the universe, one strand at a time. Socrates couldn't believe people actually had theories about strings.

Demetrios was a well-known television actor with an action-adventure series of his own. His face—and a whole lot of his bare, sculpted torso—had recently been on a billboard in Times Square. Socrates had averted his eyes and muttered, "What next?"

But he wouldn't have believed it if anyone had told him.

Yiannis, the youngest of Tallie's four older brothers, who was as city-born and -bred as the rest of them, had, five years ago, finished a master's degree in forestry and was living and working at the top of a Montana mountain!

It was Tallie who had always been determined to follow in her father's footsteps. She was the one with the head for business. She was the one who had worked in stockrooms and storerooms, in warehouses and shipping offices, doing everything she could to learn how things worked from the ground up.

And she was the one her father had fired more than once when he'd found her working in one of his companies.

"No daughter of mine is going to work here," he'd blustered and fumed.

So she'd gone to work for someone else.

He hadn't liked that any better. But Tallie was as stubborn as her old man. She'd gone to university and done a degree in accounting. She'd taken a job in California, crunching numbers for a mom-and-pop tortilla factory. And while she was there, she'd learned everything from how to make tortillas to a thousand ways to cook with them to the cleverest way to market them. Then she'd gone back and got her MBA, working on the side for a Viennese baker who taught her everything he knew. If she were ever going into business for herself, Tallie decided, it would be in baking. She loved making cakes and tortes and pastries. But she preferred that as her relaxation.

Eighteen months ago, MBA in hand, she'd applied for another job with one of her father's companies—and had been turned down.

So she'd gone to work for Easley Manufacturing, one of his biggest competitors. She'd been doing well there and had recently been promoted. She was on the fast track, the boss had told her. She'd hoped word would get back to Socrates.

Obviously it had.

Two weeks ago he'd rung and invited her to dinner after she got off work.

"Dinner?" she'd echoed. "With whom?"

Had he dredged up another eligible Greek, in other words?

"Just me," Socrates said, offended. "I'm in the city. Your mother is in Rome with her art group. I'm lonely. I thought I'd call my daughter and invite her to a meal."

It sounded perfectly innocent, but Tallie had known her father for twenty-nine years. She knew suppressed excitement when she heard it in his voice. She accepted, but not without reservations.

And when she'd met him at Lazlo's, a Hungarian restaurant on the Upper East Side he'd suggested, she had looked around warily for stray males before she went to sit at the table with him.

But Socrates hadn't come bearing Greeks for a change. Instead he'd offered her a job.

"A job?" Tallie had done her best to hide her incredulity while she found herself glancing outside to see if the late-May sun was still shining. The words h*ell froze over* were flitting around in her brain. "What sort of job?"

Her father waited until the server had brought their dinners. Then he said in his characteristic blunt fashion. "I've just acquired forty percent of Antonides Marine International. They build boats. As major stockholder, I get to name the president." He paused, smiling. "You."

"*Me?*" Tallie's voice squeaked. She blinked rapidly. Now she was sure that hell had frozen over. Or that she'd lost her mind.

But Socrates picked up his knife and fork and cut into his

chicken paprika and said with a shrug, "You've always said you wanted to come into the business."

"Yes, but—"

"So now you're in."

Tallie shook her head, mind still whirling. "I meant…I *didn't* mean I expected you to buy me a company, Dad!"

"I didn't buy you a company," he said, enunciating every word. "I acquired *part* of a company. And so, I have a say in how it's run. I want you to run it."

Tallie wet her lips. Her brain spun with possibilities, with potential—with panic. She tried to get a toehold on her thoughts. "I don't— It's so…sudden."

"The best opportunities often are."

"I know." But still…she needed to think. To consider. To—

"So, what do you say?"

"I—" Her tongue seemed welded to the roof of her mouth.

Socrates smiled gently and regarded her over a forkful of chicken. "Or maybe you were just talking. Maybe you don't think you can do it."

By God, yes, she could do it!

And she'd said so.

Socrates had beamed, the way a shark must beam when an unsuspecting little fish swims straight into his mouth. Tallie knew it. She could almost hear his jaws snap shut. But she didn't care.

Whatever agenda her father had in offering her this job, she had her own agenda—to do the best damned job she could do and prove to him that she was worthy of his trust.

The two weeks she had to spend working out her notice at Easley's had given her time to break in a replacement and do a crash course of reading everything she could get her hands on about Antonides Marine International.

What she'd learned about its history had made her even more eager to get to work. It was an old and respected boat-building company that had fallen on hard times and over the past eight years had been in the process of righting itself and moving ahead. While there was no change in leadership—Aeolus Antonides was still president (until today!)—his son had been running things. And apparently the son had done rather well. He'd economized and streamlined things, getting back to basics, redefining and refocusing the company's mission. Recently she'd read that AMI appeared poised to branch out, to test the waters in areas other than strictly marine construction. It was on the brink of expansion.

Tallie could hardly wait to be part of the process.

And now, she thought as she stood on the pavement and stared up at the old Brooklyn warehouse that was the home of the offices of Antonides Marine International, she was.

Amazingly the address was only nine blocks from her flat. She had expected some mid-Manhattan office building. Six months ago, she knew, she would have been right. But then AMI had moved across the East River to Brooklyn.

Tallie understood it was a cost-cutting move. But there was a certain rightness to it being here in DUMBO, the neighborhood acronym for its location "down under the Manhattan Bridge."

DUMBO was a vital, happening place—lots of urban renewal going on, considerable gentrification of the old brownstones and even older warehouses that sat on or near the edge of the East River. It was that energy, as well as the more reasonable rents, that had drawn her to DUMBO. She imagined it had drawn the management of AMI as well.

But looking around in the crisp early morning light, Tallie could see that it belonged here anyway, in the old five-story brick warehouse in the process of being restored. Within sight of the old Navy Shipyards, it was where a shipbuilding company—even the corporate offices thereof—ought to be.

Feng shui, her friend Katy who knew these things, would have said. Or maybe that was just inside buildings and where you put your bed. But it felt right. And that made Tallie smile and feel even better.

She was early—way early—but she couldn't wait any longer. She pushed open the door and went in.

It was like stepping across the ocean. Expecting the traditional neutral business environment, she was startled to find herself in a foyer painted blue—and not the soft pale blue one usually found on walls—but the deep vibrant blue of the Mediterranean. From floor to ceiling there was blue sea and blue sky—and dotted here and there were brown islands out of which seemed to grow impossibly white buildings and blue-domed churches. All very simple and spare, and almost breathtaking in its unexpectedness. And in it appropriateness.

Tallie had never been to the Greek homeland of her forebears. She'd never had time. But she knew it at once and found it drawing her in. Instinctively she reached out a finger and traced the line of rooftops, then a bare hillside, then one lone white building at the far end of one island. As if it were a sentry. A lookout.

She'd never particularly wanted to go to Greece. It had seemed the source of all the tradition she'd spent her life battling. But now she could see there was more to it than that. And suddenly the notion tempted her.

But not as much as punching the elevator button and hitting 3.

The elevator was apparently part of the refurbishment, all polished wood and carpet that still smelled new. When the door slid open three floors later she saw that the renovation was still a work in progress. The floor was bare, unfinished wood. The walls were plastered but unpainted. She could hear hammering coming from behind a closed door down the hall.

She thought briefly that whoever was doing it, she'd have to get his name and pass it on to her landlord. Arnie was trying to get some renovations done on one of the apartments and couldn't find a workman who would show up before noon.

She passed several offices—an accountant, a magazine publisher, a dentist—before she found the new heavy glass door of Antonides Marine International. The door was locked. At six-forty in the morning she could hardly expect otherwise.

No matter. She had a key. A key to her company. Well, a key to the company she was president of.

Now all she had to do was prove herself worthy of it.

Taking a deep breath and feeling the rightness of the moment, Tallie set her briefcase down and shifted the bag in her arm to get out the key. Then she turned it in the lock, pushed open the door and went in.

She was late.

First day on the job and the new hotshot president of Antonides Marine couldn't even be bothered to show up!

Elias prowled his office, coffee mug in hand, grinding the teeth with which he'd intended to take a bite out of her. So much for the "eager beaver" his father had assured him Socrates insisted she was.

He supposed he ought to be pleased. If she wasn't there, she couldn't screw things up. He'd spent the past two weeks trying to make sure she had as little opportunity to interfere as possible.

Once it had been clear that there was no way out of the mess his father had created, Elias had done his best to limit the damage. That meant defining the limits of the problem and making sure it didn't get bigger. So he'd readied the big office overlooking the river—the one he'd hoped to move into someday but which was too far from the hub of the office to be practical now. That was for when things were running themselves.

Or for when he was running them and needed to stick a figurehead president as far from the action as possible, he thought grimly. With her conveniently out of the way, he could get on with running the company. Which he ought to be doing right now, damn it! But he wanted her settled and disposed of first.

He had expected she'd at least be there by nine, but it was already half past. He'd been at his desk since eight, ready to deal with the interloper. Rosie, his assistant, had been there when he came in and had coffee brewing—obviously trying to impress the new "boss."

She told him to make his own damn coffee on a daily basis. She'd even put a plate of fancy cookies by the coffeemaker.

Elias had considered giving her grief over them, but they

were damn good. Some buttery chocolate kind with a hint of cinnamon, and some with almonds, and the traditional American favorite, peanut butter criss-cross.

His stomach growled now just thinking about them, and he went out to snatch another one only to find everyone else already there.

His normally spit-and-polished researcher, Paul Johanssen, was talking with his mouth full. Lucy, who oversaw the contracts and accounting, was deciding to go on her diet tomorrow. Dyson, who did blueprints and development for AMI projects, had crumbs in his mustache, and even the temp steno girls, Trina and Cara and the very-pregnant-and-about-to-deliver-any-moment Giulia were sneaking into reception to steal a cookie or two.

Elias thought it was no wonder Rosie had always refused to even make coffee in the office. If they'd known the extent of her talents, they wouldn't have let her do anything else.

Well, Ms Thalia Savas was sure to be impressed—provided she managed to show up before the coffee and cookies were gone.

But he was done waiting. It was time she realized this wasn't business school. Real work got done in the real world.

"We'll go into the boardroom," he said to Paul and Dyson. They jumped guiltily at the sound of his voice, and Paul surreptitiously wiped his mouth.

Elias grinned, taking a bit of perverse satisfaction in the tardy Ms Savas missing out on the cookies made especially for her. Not to mention that Rosie had gone to all that trouble only to have her efforts gobbled up by the rest of the staff.

"Very impressive," he said as he passed her on his way to the boardroom. "I can see why you don't do it all the time."

Rosie looked up. "I didn't do it at all."

Elias gave her a sceptical look, but she stared him down so sternly that he turned to Paul. "Don't tell me you baked them?"

Paul laughed. "I can't boil water."

"Don't look at me," Dyson backed away, shaking his dreadlocks and grinning.

"Maybe the new girl made them," Trina suggested as she headed back to her office with her arms full of files.

"What new girl?" Elias knew they were going to send one to fill Giulia's spot, but he didn't know she'd arrived.

"I guess that would be me." A cheerful, unfamiliar voice from the hallway made them all turn around. She was not the usual temp agency girl. She was older for one thing. Late twenties probably. She didn't resemble a stick insect, either. She was slender but definitely curvy. She also wasn't wearing a nose ring or sporting a hank of blue hair. Her hair, in fact, though pulled back and tied down and even anchored, had a will of its own. And even the army of barrettes she'd enlisted to tame it wasn't up to the job. Her hair was thick and wild and decidedly sexy.

She looked as if she'd just got out of bed.

Elias found himself imagining what she would be like *in* bed. The thought brought him up short. He was as appreciative of a beautiful woman as the next man, but he didn't usually fantasize about taking them to bed within moments of meeting them.

Then Ms Temp smiled brightly at him, at the same time giving her head a little shake so that her hair actually danced. And the urge to pull out those pins and tangle his fingers in that glorious hair hit him harder.

He shoved his hands in his pockets. He knew better than to mix business and pleasure.

"*You* made the cookies?" he demanded.

She nodded, still smiling. "Did you like them?"

"They're good," he acknowledged gruffly. But he didn't want her getting the idea she could use them as a ticket to something more. "But they aren't necessary. You only have to do your job."

"My job?" She looked blank.

So she had a temp brain apparently. "Filing," he said patiently. "Typing. Doing what you're told."

"I don't type. I hate to file. And I rarely do what I'm told," she said cheerfully.

Elias frowned. "Then what the hell are you doing here?"

She stuck out her hand to shake his. "I'm Tallie Savas. The new president. It's nice to meet you."

# CHAPTER TWO

DAMN Socrates, anyway.

One look at Elias Antonides and Tallie knew she'd been had. So much for her father finally taking her seriously.

Now she knew what he was really up to. The presidency of Antonides Marine was nothing more than a means to throw her into the path of a Greek god in khakis and a blue oxford cloth shirt.

Elias Antonides was definitely that—an astonishingly handsome Greek god with thick, wavy, tousled black hair, a wide mobile mouth, strong cheekbones and an aquiline nose that was no less attractive for having been rearranged at some earlier date. Its slight crook only made him look tough and capable—like the sort of god who could quell sea monsters on the one hand while sacking Troy on the other.

And naturally he wasn't wearing a wedding ring, which just confirmed her suspicions. Well, she certainly couldn't say her father didn't have high aspirations.

But he must have lost his mind to imagine that a hunk like Elias Antonides would be interested in *her!*

In the looks department, Tallie knew she was decidedly average. Passable, but certainly not head-turning. Some men liked her hair, but they rarely liked the high-energy, high-powered brain beneath it. More men liked her father's money, but they seldom wanted to put up with a woman who had a mind of her own.

Only Brian had loved her for herself. And until she found another man who did, she wasn't interested.

When the right man came along, he wouldn't be intimidated by her brain or attracted only by her hair or her father's millions. He would love her.

He certainly wouldn't be looking at her, appalled, as Elias Antonides was, like she was something nasty he'd found on the bottom of his shoe. At least she didn't have to worry that Elias was in on her father's little game.

But if he found her presence so distasteful, why hadn't he just told her father—and his—no? As managing director—not to mention the man who had pulled Antonides Marine back from the edge of the financial abyss over the past eight years—surely he had some say in the matter.

Maybe he was just always surly.

Well, Tallie wasn't surly, and she was determined to make the best of this as a business opportunity, regardless of what her father's hidden agenda was.

So she grabbed Elias's hand and shook it firmly. "You must be Elias. I'm glad to meet you at last. And I'm glad you liked the cookies. I thought I should begin as I mean to go on."

"Making cookies?" He stared at her as if she'd lost her mind, then scowled, his brow furrowing, which would have made the average man look baffled and confused. It made Elias Antonides look brooding and dangerous and entirely too tempting. Silently Tallie cursed her father.

"Yes," she said firmly. "I've always found that people like them—and so they enjoy coming to work."

Elias's brows lifted, and he looked down his patrician nose at her. "Enjoyment is highly overrated, Ms Savas," he said haughtily.

Tallie let out a sigh of relief. Oh, good, if he was going to be all stiff and pompous, he would be much easier to resist.

"Oh, I don't agree at all," she said frankly. "I think it's enormously important. If employee morale is low," she informed him, "the business suffers."

His teeth came together with a snap. "Morale at Antonides Marine is not low."

"Of course it isn't," Tallie agreed. "And I want to keep it that way."

"Cookies do not make morale."

"Well, they don't hurt," she said. "And they certainly improve the quality of life, don't you think?" She glanced around at the group who had been scarfing down her best offering and was gratified to see several heads nod vigorously.

A glare from Elias brought them to an abrupt halt. "Don't you have work to do?" he asked them.

The heads bobbed again, and the group started to scatter.

"Before you go, though," Tallie said. "I'd like to meet you."

Elias didn't look pleased, but he stuffed his hands in his pockets and stood silently while she introduced herself to each one, shook hands and tried to commit all their names to memory.

Paul was blond and bespectacled and crew-cut and personified efficiency. "I hope you'll be very happy here," he told her politely.

Dyson was black with flying dreadlocks and a gold hoop earring. "You're good for my morale," he told her with a grin, and snagged another cookie.

Rosie was short and curvy with flame-coloured hair. It was her job, she said, to keep everyone in line. "Even him." She jerked her head at Elias. "I never make coffee," she told Tallie. "Or cookies." Then she confided that she might—if she could have these recipes.

"Sure, no problem," Tallie said.

Lucy wore her silver hair in a bun and had a charm bracelet with a charm for every grandchild. Trina had long black hair with one blue streak, while Cara's was short and spiky and decidedly pink. Giulia looked as if she were going to deliver triplets any minute.

"Boy or girl?" Tallie asked her.

"Boy," Giulia said. "And soon, I hope," she added wearily. "I want to see my feet."

Tallie laughed. "My friend Katy said the same thing."

They were a nice group, she decided after she'd chatted with them all. Friendly, welcoming. Everyone said they were happy to have her. Well, everyone except Elias Antonides.

He never said a word.

Finally, when the group began to head back to their various jobs, she looked at him. He was studying her as if she were a bomb he had to defuse.

"Perhaps we should talk?" she suggested. "Get acquainted?"

"Perhaps we should," he said, his voice flat. He raked a hand through his hair, then sighed and called after Paul and Dyson, "Just keep going on the Corbett project. We'll meet later."

"If you need to meet with them, don't let me interrupt," Tallie said.

"I won't."

No, not really very welcoming at all.

But Tallie persisted, determined to get a spark of interest out of him. "I apologize for not letting you know I was already here," she said. "I came in about seven. I could hardly wait," she confided. "I was always getting to school on the first day hours early, too. Do you do that?"

"No."

Right. Okay, let's take a different tack.

"I found my office. Thank you for the name plaque, by the way. I don't think I've ever had a plaque before. And thank you for all the fiscal reports. I got them from my father, so I'd already read them and I have a few questions. For example, have you considered that Corbett's, while a viable possible acquisition, might not be the best one to start with? I thought—"

"Look, Ms Savas," he said abruptly, "this isn't going to work."

"What isn't going to work?"

"This! This question-and-answer business! You baking cookies, for God's sake, then coming in with questions concerning things you know nothing about! I don't have time for it. I have a business to run."

"A business I am president of," she reminded him archly.

"On account of a bet."

Tallie stopped dead. "Bet? What bet?"

Hard dark eyes met hers accusingly. "You don't know?"

But before she could do more than begin to shake her head, his jaw tightened and he sighed. "No, probably you don't." He opened his mouth, then shut it again. "Not here," he muttered, glancing around the open break room. "Come on."

And he grabbed her arm, steered her out the door and down the hallway, past the chattering temps and his flame-haired, goggle-eyed secretary and straight into his office. He shut the door with a definite click.

Elias Antonides's office was far smaller than the one he'd given her. It didn't even have a window. It had a desk overflowing with papers and files, two filing cabinets, a blueprint cabinet, three bookcases and one glorious wall painted by the same artist who had done the murals in the entry downstairs.

"Wow," Tallie said involuntarily.

Elias looked startled. "Wow?"

She nodded at the mural. "It's unexpected. Breathtaking. You don't need a window."

"No." He stared at the mural a long moment, his jaw tight. Then abruptly he turned his gaze back to her and gestured toward a chair. "Sit down."

It was more a command than an invitation. But it didn't seem worth fighting about, so Tallie sat, then waited for him to do likewise. But he didn't. He cracked his knuckles and paced behind his desk. A muscle worked in his jaw. He opened his mouth to speak, then stopped, paced some more and finally came to a stop directly behind the desk where at last he turned to face her. But he still didn't speak.

"The bet?" Tallie prompted, not sure she wanted to know this, but reasonably certain it would shed light on why Elias was so upset.

"My father fancies himself a racing sailor," he said at last. "And after he sold forty percent of Antonides Marine without telling anyone of his intentions—"

Uh-oh.

"—he hadn't screwed things up badly enough yet. So he and

your father made a little bet." Elias cracked his knuckles again. She got the feeling he wished he was cracking his father's head.

"What sort of bet?" Tallie asked warily. Dear God, her father hadn't bet her hand in marriage, had he? He hadn't done anything quite that outrageous yet in his attempt to marry her off, but she wouldn't put it past him.

"The winner got the other's island house and the presidency of Antonides Marine."

"But that's ridiculous!" Tallie protested. "What on earth would my father want with another house?" He had five now— if you counted what the family called "the hermitage" on a little island off the coast of Maine.

"I have no idea," Elias said grimly. "I don't think the houses had anything to do with it…even though," he added bitterly, "in our case it was our family's home for generations."

"So why did they do it? Because of the presidency?"

Elias shrugged. "Not my father."

But hers would have cared a great deal, she thought. She didn't say so, however. "Then why would your father bet?"

"Because he thought he'd win!" Elias's dark eyes flashed in anger. He shoved his hands through his hair. "He likes a good challenge. Especially when he's got what he considers a sure thing. He didn't count on your brother, the Olympic sailor," Elias added heavily. He flung himself down in his chair and glared at her as if it were her fault.

Tallie knew whose fault it was. "Oh, dear. Daddy got Theo to race."

It wasn't a question. Of course he had got Theo to race— because just like Aeolus Antonides, Socrates Savas *always* played to win. And in this case, Aeolus had something that Socrates wanted far more than any house—the presidency for his daughter—and the consequent proximity to Aeolus's Greek godson.

At least he hadn't offered her hand in marriage.

But what he had done was almost worse.

"Then we'll just call it off," Tallie said firmly. As much as she wanted the chance to prove herself, she was damned if she wanted the opportunity this way. "I'll quit and you can have your house back."

Elias looked surprised at her suggestion. Then he surprised *her* by shaking his head. "Won't work."

"Why not?"

"Because it's your father's. He won it, fair and square." Elias's mouth twisted as he said that. "Or as fair as Socrates Savas is likely to be."

"My father doesn't cheat!" Tallie defended her father fiercely on that count. He manipulated with the best of them. He played all the angles, pushed the edges of the envelope. But he didn't cheat.

Elias shrugged. "Whatever. He's got the house. And he's going to keep the house."

"I'll tell him not to. If I can't hand it back to you, I'll quit. I won't take the job."

"You have to take the job."

"Why?"

"Because that's the deal. That's the only way he'll deed it back."

Deals? Bets? She wanted to strangle her father.

"Tell me," she said grimly.

"He told my father he'd deed it back in two years…" Elias stopped and shook his head.

"If…?" Tallie prompted. She knew there was an *if*. There was always an *if*.

Elias ground his teeth. "If I stay on as managing director of Antonides," Elias said at last. "And you stay on as president."

"For *two* years?"

Obviously her father didn't have much confidence in her if he figured she would need two years to get Elias to the altar, Tallie thought wryly. Or maybe he thought it would take him two years to convince her that it was a good idea.

It *wasn't* a good idea. And she had no intention of doing any such thing!

"That's absurd," she said at last. "We don't have to play their games."

"The house—"

"It can't be that great a house!" she objected.

"There are a thousand others like it," he agreed readily.

"Well then—"

Elias steepled his hands. "My father was born there. His father was born there. His grandfather was born there. The only reason I wasn't born there was because my folks came to New York the year before I was born. But generations of Antonides have lived and loved and died in that house. We go back all the time. I built boats with my grandfather there when I was a boy." There was no tonelessness in his voice now. All the emotion he had so carefully reined in earlier was ragged in his voice now. "My parents were married there, for God's sake! It's our history, our heart."

"Then your father had no business *betting* it." Tallie was almost as mad at his father as he was.

"Of course he didn't! And your father had no business taking advantage of a man who shouldn't be let out alone."

They glared at each other.

It was true, Tallie reflected, what Elias just said. Her father had always had an eye for the main chance. His own dirt-poor immigrant parents had taught him that. If the Antonides family had an ancestral home to lose, it was more than Socrates's family had ever had. Tallie had been brought up on stories of how hard they'd worked for little pay. So when opportunities came along, you took them, Socrates said. And luck—well, that you made yourself.

Tallie didn't doubt for a minute that her father thought taking advantage of Aeolus Antonides was a prime bit of luck.

"So what do you propose we do?" she asked politely, since she had no doubt he'd tell her anyway.

"I don't propose *we* do anything," Elias said sharply. "I've been doing just fine for the past eight years on my own. I've pulled Antonides Marine out of the red, I've made it profitable, and I'll continue to do so. And since you have to be here, Ms

President, you can sit in your office or you can bake cookies—
or file your fingernails."

"I'm *not* going to be filing my fingernails!"

"Whatever. Just stay out of my way."

She gaped at him. "I'm the president!"

"You're an interloper," Elias said flatly. "Why'd your old man
stick you in here anyway?"

Tallie coloured, certain she knew the real reason. But it wasn't
the one she gave him. "Because I can do the job!"

That was the truth, just not all of it.

Elias snorted. "You don't know a damned thing about the marine business."

"I'm learning. I read every report my father sent. I researched
AMI in journals and business weeklies. I spent the morning read-
ing the financial statements you put in my office. And I told you
I have some concerns—"

"Which are not necessary."

"On the contrary, they are. If Antonides Marine is going to
move out of strictly boat building, I think we should be considering a variety of options—"

"Which I have done."

"—and we need to examine the whole marketing strategy—"

"Which I have done."

"—before we make a decision."

"And I will make a decision."

Once more they glared at each other.

"Look," Tallie said finally, mustering every bit of patience she
could manage. "We both agree that I can't leave—for our own
reasons," she added quickly, before he could speak. "So I'm
staying. And since I am, I'm getting involved. I'm president of
Antonides Marine, whether you like it or not. And I won't be
shunted aside. I won't let you do it."

Elias's jaw worked. He glowered at her. Tallie glowered right
back. And they might have gone right on glowering if the phone
hadn't rung.

Elias snatched it up. "What?" he barked.

Whatever the answer was, it didn't please him. He listened, drummed his fingers on the desktop, then ground his teeth. "Yeah, okay. Put her through." He punched the hold button and looked at Tallie. "It's my sister. I have to talk to her."

From the look on his face, Tallie didn't think she'd want to be Elias Antonides's sister right now. Or any other time for that matter.

"Fine," she said. "Go right ahead."

She needed time to come to terms with the things she'd learned this morning, anyway. It was far worse than she'd thought—the bet, the house, the deal, the arrogant unsuspecting Greek god her father had his eye on as a prospective son-in-law, not to mention said Greek god's "file your fingernails" attitude about what her role should be at Antonides Marine. Oh, yes, she had her work cut out for her.

She stood up. "I'll be in my office if you need me."

"Yeah, that'll happen," Elias muttered.

She shot him a hard look, but he was already back on the telephone with his sister.

"No," Elias said.

It was what he always said to Cristina. It wasn't the bead shop this time. As he'd suspected, that had been a momentary whim. But this conversation wasn't going any better. Whenever he talked to his sister Cristina, they ended up at loggerheads. Usually it happened sooner. Like within a minute.

This time it had taken ten, but mostly because he was distracted, his mind still playing over the frustrating encounter with Ms President while Cristina rabbited on about how she'd been out sailing off Montauk last week, and wasn't it beautiful at Montauk this time of year, and on and on.

Waiting for her to get to the point, Elias had tried to think how he could have handled the irritatingly sanguine Ms Savas differently. Surely there had to be some way to convince her to leave well enough alone and not meddle in Antonides Marine affairs. But he couldn't think of one.

She'd flat-out said, "I don't follow directions well," and then she'd pretty much proved it. Annoying woman!

"It was a beaut," Cristina enthused. "You'd love it. You should come with us next time."

Elias dragged his brain back from Tallie Savas long enough to say, "No time."

"Oh, for heaven's sake, Elias. Get a life."

"I have a life," Elias said stiffly, even though he was sure Cristina wouldn't consider working seventy hours a week on Antonides Marine and another thirty or forty renovating the building much of a life at all.

"Sure you do." Cristina sniffed. "Come on, Elias. Mark would love to take you."

So she was still with Mark? After what—two months now? Elias supposed it was some sort of record.

"You could bring Gretl," she suggested enthusiastically. "We saw her this weekend, Mark and I. I don't know why you dumped her."

And he wasn't going to tell her, either.

When he'd met Gretl Gustavsson at a South Street Seaport bar one night, she'd just broken up with her boyfriend and had no interest in getting serious again anytime soon. As Elias had no interest in getting serious at all, they'd enjoyed each other's company.

Their relationship, which Elias didn't even want to describe with that word, had gone on for the past two years—until Gretl started acting as if there was more to it than there was.

"I've wasted two years on you, Elias," she'd told him a couple of months ago.

Elias hadn't considered them a waste, but if that was the way she wanted to look at it, so be it. He'd said goodbye, and that was that. He hadn't seen her since.

"She's so sweet. She asked about you." Cristina waited hopefully and got no response. She sighed. "Well, if you don't want Gretl, fine. We'll find you someone else."

"No, you won't," Elias said sharply. "I don't need you setting me up with a woman. Besides, I'm busy. I've got work up to my eyebrows. And it just got harder. In case you haven't heard, we have a new president of Antonides Marine."

"Daddy told me. And it's a woman!" Amazement didn't even begin to cover Cristina's feelings about that. She giggled. "Do you think *he's* setting you up?"

"No, I damned well don't!" Though the thought had certainly occurred to him. Still, his father was rarely that subtle. Aeolus took a more shove-the-woman-in-his-face approach.

And the truth was, Tallie Savas would never be his father's choice in a woman.

Aeolus loved his wife, but he had never stopped ogling tall, big-busted Nordic beauties. He'd thought Gretl was stunning, which she had been. But Elias had never fantasized going to bed with her. Because he'd *gone* to bed with her, he told himself. There had never been any speculation. Never any mystery with Gretl.

Whereas with Tallie Savas and her miles of wild curly hair—

"Maybe I'll come and check her out. What's she like?" Cristina said eagerly.

"Nothing special." Elias made sure his tone was dampening. Then he cleared his throat. "She's an MBA. A CEO. All business."

"Battle-ax, hmm?"

"Pretty much."

"Oh." Cristina's disappointment was obvious. "I wonder what Daddy was thinking then."

"I doubt he *was* thinking."

Cristina laughed. "He's not that bad, Elias. He likes Mark."

"Which proves my case."

"It does not," Cristina said, but she didn't sound as defensive as she usually did about her boyfriends. "You don't know him. He knows a lot about boats. If the lady prez is a hard worker, you'll have some time off now. You can come out with Mark and me."

"No." Which brought them back to where they'd started. Elias pinched the bridge of his nose. "Look, Cristina, I've got work to do—"

"You won't even meet him," she accused.

"I've met him," Elias said wearily. "I went to Yale with him."

"So I heard. He said he's changed since Yale."

Elias hoped so. At Yale Mark had been a drunken reveler who'd only got in because his father knew someone who knew someone. What was it with Greek fathers?

"If you want me to meet him again, bring him out to the folks' on Sunday." He'd managed to avoid his mother's last Sunday dinner by pleading a work overload. He wasn't going to get out of this one and he knew it.

"I'm not sure that's a good idea," Cristina mumbled.

"I thought you said the old man liked him."

"Yes, but only because he can beat Mark at golf."

Elias laughed. "Well, there you go. Something to build on. You'll work it out, Crissie. I have to go. I'll see you Sunday."

"I'll bring Mark if you bring Ms President."

"Goodbye, Crissie." Elias hung up before his sister got any more bright ideas.

He had other far more important things to deal with—like convincing Thalia Savas, aka Ms President, that despite what she thought, it was a better idea to spend the next two years filing her fingernails than trying to meddle in the business of Antonides Marine.

If she thought she'd done her homework, Elias thought, rubbing his hands together in anticipation, she had another think coming.

He'd show her homework. And he knew exactly where to start.

"For me?" Tallie looked up and smiled brightly when Elias appeared in her office late that afternoon with a three-foot-high-stack of reports and folders.

"For you," Elias agreed cheerfully, thumping them on her desk. "Since you want to be involved in the decisions, you'll want to get up to speed.

"Of course I will," she agreed promptly. "Thank you very much."

He gave her a hard-eyed gaze, but she smiled in the face of it and finally he just shrugged. "My pleasure." He turned toward the door, then paused and glanced back. "I'll have more for you tomorrow."

Tallie's determined smile didn't waver. "I can hardly wait."

In fact, she was having a very good time. After he'd finished his phone call with his sister, he'd gone into the boardroom to meet with Paul and Dyson. He hadn't invited her, but she had gone in anyway. He'd looked startled when she'd opened the door and very much like he'd like to throw her out. But finally he'd shrugged and said, "Pull up a chair."

Tallie had pulled up a chair and taken out a notepad and pen. She'd listened intently, making notes but not saying a word, though from the way Elias angled a glance at her periodically, she knew he was expecting her to stick her oar in.

She never did.

The first order of business she'd learned from her father was to look and listen before saying anything at all. It had stood her in good stead before. She intended to do the same thing here.

Listening today was quite enough. She was impressed with how thorough Elias was and how he was able to take the information Paul provided and examine it from different angles. He had, as he'd told her, done a thorough job of considering many of the ramifications of the purchase of Corbett's.

She still wasn't convinced that it was a good move. It seemed a little too far afield, but she would listen and consider and do more work on her own, and then she'd comment.

In the meantime, she'd read the stack of material he left her.

She wouldn't have been surprised if he'd given her three feet of invoices and grocery lists to read. But she wouldn't know unless she skimmed every single piece. So she spent the rest of the afternoon in her office doing just that.

Some of the reports seemed little more than she'd expected. But some were significant. They outlined in far greater detail than the material her father had given her what the financial status of Antonides Marine had been when Elias had come in eight years ago—and what it was now.

She got a far clearer understanding of just how dire the straits had been when Elias had taken over, and an even greater appreciation for how astute his business handling was. He'd seen what needed to be done, and he'd done it—even when it had meant cutting out some very appealing but not terribly lucrative lines.

The venture into luxury yacht construction that his father had spent vast amounts on was obviously one of Aeolus's pet projects. It had drained the company's assets, though, and had brought in very little.

When Elias took over, it had been the first thing to go.

There was nothing in the papers he gave her that spelled out in words his father's opposition. But in the "who was in favor of what" pieces, it was clear that Elias's decision had met with considerable parental opposition.

She wondered if she dared point it out to him as something the two of them had in common. Somehow she doubted it. But the more she read, the less she blamed him for his attitude. And when at last she leaned back in her chair and contemplated the skyline of Manhattan against the setting sun, she had to admit that if she were Elias Antonides, she'd resent an interloper coming in, too.

At eight o'clock when she gathered up the stack of papers she intended to take home for further study. It was a foot and a half high, but every bit could be all important. When she finally opened her mouth, she wanted to have her facts straight. Giving the stack a little pat, she went in search of a box to put it in.

The office was deserted. Rosie had left ages ago, but not without poking her head in to remind Tallie to bring the recipes tomorrow.

She'd promised them to Paul, too, who thought his fiancée would like them, and to Dyson who'd said he didn't have a fiancée, but who needed one? If you wanted cookies badly enough—and they were good enough—you just baked them yourself.

"I'm liberated," he'd told Tallie.

She smiled now at the memory, glad she'd brought them, determined to bring others tomorrow. They were good for morale.

And they were an excellent way to connect with the staff, even if some people, she thought as she opened the supply closet, looked down their once-broken noses at them.

"Ah, excellent," she muttered, discovering a box behind the paper supplies. She fished it out, then stood up and turned, slamming into a hard male chest.

"Can I help you find something?" Elias's tone was polite, his meaning was anything but. Loosely translated, Tallie knew, he wanted to know what the hell she was doing.

She smiled brightly at him. "You're still here, too? I was just getting a box to take some work home." She tried to step around him.

He blocked her way. "What work?"

"Some of that reading material you provided. Excuse me." Her tone was polite, too, but when he didn't move, she side-stepped him and—accidentally, of course—knocked the box into his solar plexis. "Oh! Sorry."

Not exactly the truth, but if he was going to stand in her way… She heard him mutter under his breath as she hurried back down the hall with the box in her arms.

Footsteps came after her. "You don't need to take things home." He stopped in the door of her office, scowling as she piled the papers into the box.

"Well, I don't plan to stay here all night."

"You're taking way too much trouble."

"It's not trouble. It's my job."

His jaw bunched, and she knew he was itching to say, "No, it's mine."

But he didn't say anything, just exhaled sharply and rocked back on his heels before muttering something under his breath, then turning and stalking off down the hall.

"Welcome to your first wonderful day at Antonides Marine," Tallie murmured to herself as she watched him stalk away.

No question about it—Tallie Savas was going to be a pain.

Who the hell needed a president who baked cookies? Who came to meetings and sat there, scribbling furiously on a notepad and never said a word? Who buried herself in her office with the piles and piles of reports he'd given her and actually read them? *And* took them home with her?

Elias stood glaring after her from his office as she tottered toward the door, the box full of files balanced on top of her briefcase, and three empty cookie tins teetering precariously on top of that.

A gentleman would help her with it.

Elias didn't feel much like a gentleman. He would have liked to have seen her collapse in a heap.

But the way his life was going at the moment, his father would probably want to pay all her medical bills with money Elias hadn't made yet!

Grimly he strode after her. "Allow me," he said with frigid politeness and opened the door for her.

"Thanks." She gave him a sweet smile that was completely at odds with her stubborn refusal to go home and let him get on with the job. "Have a good evening."

"Oh, yeah," he said drily.

She turned her head to grin at him. The top cookie tin teetered, and she nearly dropped them all, rescuing it.

Against his better judgment, Elias said grudgingly, "Do you want some help?"

Tallie shook her head—and the cookie tins and the briefcase and the box. "No, thanks." And she wobbled off down the hall.

Oddly annoyed at having his offer refused, Elias shut the door behind her. But he didn't move away. He continued to watch her through the glass. If she dropped the damn things, she'd have to let him help her.

But at that moment one of the doors down the hall opened and a man came out. Elias recognized Martin de Boer instantly from his tweedy elbow-patched jacket and his floppy earnest-and-intense-journalist-too-busy-to-get-a-haircut hair.

Martin wrote for the snooty monthly opinion mag, *Issues and Answers,* that rented a group of offices down the hall. When Elias had leased to them, he'd figured they'd be congenial tenants, and the people who worked on the physical magazine were. He even played recreational league basketball with the layout director.

But the journalists who wrote for *Issues and Answers* were a different story. They thought everyone else had issues but only they had answers. And from the few conversations Elias had had with him, Martin de Boer had more answers than most. As far as Elias could see, de Boer was a pompous, arrogant know-it-all who stuck his oar in where it wasn't needed.

And his opinion didn't improve as he watched Martin smile and speak to Tallie, obviously offering to help carry her box. In this case he got a brilliant smile in return and a reply that permitted him to whisk the box out of her arms gallantly and cradle it in his own.

Hell! Elias glared. She'd practically kicked his shins when he'd offered! He was half tempted to stalk down the hall and jerk the damn box out of de Boer's skinny arms.

Good thing his cell phone rang.

Bad thing to hear his father's voice, jovial and upbeat, booming down the line. "Well how'd it go today with our new president?"

Elias, watching Tallie disappear into the elevator with Martin the Bore, bit out two words: "Don't ask."

# CHAPTER THREE

THE PHONE began ringing right after she came in the door.

"Just wanted to see how things went," Socrates said. Her father's tone was deliberately casual and offhand but at the same time simply simmering with curiosity.

Tallie, who was feeding a very hungry and indignant cat who thought he should have eaten two hours before, scooped some fishy-smelling glop onto a plate and set it on the floor. Harvey fell on it ravenously. She straightened and took a deep breath. "Just fine."

She would have left it at that, but she knew from experience that that wasn't the way to handle Socrates. Less was never more with her father. And letting him ask questions was worse than telling him more than enough to lead him astray.

So she launched into a full-scale report on almost everything—about the office, the murals, the furniture, the history of Antonides Marine—in short, more about the history of Antonides Marine than she was sure he ever wanted to know.

And about everything, in other words, except what she knew he wanted to hear.

To give him credit, he waited patiently through the whole recitation. It was his gift, she thought, knowing when to pounce. She made sure she gave him nothing to pounce on.

"Well, well. You certainly seem to have had a good day," he said heartily when she finally wound down. Harvey had long since finished his dinner and was eyeing the bacon and eggs she was making for herself.

Tallie shook her head and gave him a stern look. He gave her a gimlet-eyed glare that reminded her uncannily of Elias's hard-eyed stare, the one that said Antonides Marine was *his,* not hers.

My eggs. My bacon, she mouthed at him silently.

"So you like them?" Socrates pressed on in her ear. "The people? Companies are made of people, Thalia. What about the people?"

A small nudge to get her closer to what he wanted to know.

So Tallie obediently rattled on about the people. She started with Dyson: "an absolutely charming naval architect," and went on to Paul: "obviously has a strong work ethic. Solid midwestern values," and then to Rosie, Lucy, the accountant and even the temp girls. She talked and talked about everyone but—

"And Aeolus's son?" he finally had to ask. "Elias was there, wasn't he?"

"Elias? Oh, yes," Tallie agreed, as determinedly offhand as her father, damn it. "Elias was there."

Foaming at the mouth. Furious that you bet his daft father our piddly island getaway against their ancestral home, and then got Theo to make sure you won it—and the presidency to boot.

"Ah, good. And he was…helpful?" There was a certain guardedness in Socrates's tone now.

"He gave me a lot to read." Which was nothing but the truth.

"To read?"

"Reports. On the business."

"Oh. Oh, good. So he, ah, seemed to accept you, then?"

"As president, you mean?" Tallie said guilelessly. Then, "Apparently you didn't give him any choice, Dad."

Her tone told him she was onto him.

"Oh, now, that's not true!" Socrates blustered.

"Yeah, right. You didn't use Theo to get what you wanted? And tack on the presidency, as well, and then tell Aeolus Antonides that you'd deed his ancestral home back to him if—and only if—Elias remained on as managing director for two years?"

There was a minute's silence while her father apparently tried to figure out how to handle the damage control that was clearly necessary.

"I did it for you, Thalia. It is an opportunity for you. You've always wanted to go into business!" he said at last.

"As if that was the real reason you did it."

Socrates sputtered and muttered, but no words came out.

"Stop trying to manipulate my life, Dad," Tallie said evenly. "Stop trying to shove men down my throat."

"I never! I merely provided an—"

"Eligible man," Tallie filled in for him.

"So he is eligible? So what? I cannot make you marry him, can I? Or vice versa."

"But you would if you could."

There was another pause. Then, "Marriage is a wonderful thing," Socrates said. "Your mother and I—"

"Are meant for each other." And a good thing, too. Tallie couldn't imagine her parents with anyone else. " No one else would put up with you," she told him. "And I'm very happy you and Mom have each other. And if Brian had lived, I would have married him, but—"

. "He would not want you to stay single forever, Thalia."

"I know that! But he wouldn't want me to marry just anyone, either!"

"Of course not. But—"

"Stop it, Dad. Just stop."

There was a long pause, then: "I am stopped."

Yeah, right.

"We'll see," she murmured. Then she said briskly, "I have to go now, Dad. I have a lot of work to do. All that reading Elias gave me to do."

"Oh, yes?" Socrates shifted gears right along with her. "Yes. Good. I've been concerned about Antonides' intention to diversify."

So he hadn't bought the company only to shove her down Elias's throat and vice versa? He was actually interested in the business. Tallie shouldn't have been surprised. Her father never ignored the bottom line.

"I hear he is considering a buy-out of another company," Socrates said. "Tell me about it. I might know the men in this other company. What did you say it was?"

"I didn't."

There was a brief silence which Tallie didn't fill. "And what is it?" her father finally asked.

"I can't say."

"Can't say? What do you mean, you can't say?" Socrates was clearly surprised by that.

"Business is business. What goes on in the office is confidential. You know that, Dad. You taught me it yourself."

"Yes, yes. Confidential. Business is confidential. But, Thalia, not when I *own* forty percent of it!"

"Even then," Tallie said firmly. "You're on the board. You're not involved in the day-to-day running of the company."

"But—"

"No one wants to have the board second-guessing their every move. You would hate it."

"Yes, but—"

"Come to the next shareholders' meeting, Dad," she said sweetly. "We'll tell you everything you need to know there."

It was no big deal, Elias told himself every morning. So Tallie Savas's name was now on the letterhead as president of Antonides Marine.

So what? It didn't make any difference to the way he ran things.

But the truth of the matter was, it did.

It wasn't that Dyson and Paul were "yes" men. It was that they didn't see things the same way Tallie did. Dyson was theoretical and Paul was nuts and bolts. And Tallie was…well, Tallie.

She saw things from a different perspective.

"A woman's perspective," she said with a shrug, as if it, too, was no big deal.

But irritatingly, it was. She brought up things he didn't pay as much attention to—people things, like how to balance job and family issues.

Balance was not something Elias was familiar with. When he was at work, he thought about work. When he wasn't at work, he thought about work.

"Work matters. Pure and simple," he told her.

"Get a life," she told him.

They glared at each other.

But the truth was, for the first time in years, Elias found that he was having to cope with a distraction. Of course, he could claim that the distraction was work by another name—but work had never had a woman attached to it before.

And this one was definitely distracting.

Elias was ordinarily happy to appreciate a beautiful woman. But he had always—until now—been able to choose the time and place. He had never mixed business with pleasure. He was still trying not to.

It wasn't easy.

Now, at the damnedest, most inconvenient times, he'd be sitting there in a meeting, trying to focus on what Paul or Dyson was saying and he'd glance across the room at Tallie. And his attention would take a sharp turn away from the work at hand.

He would find himself transfixed by those wayward strands of hair that had a habit of escaping from the confines of whatever she was trying to tame them with that day. And the next thing he knew, he would be imagining what it would be like to see her hair untamed, wild and glorious. And it was a quick jump to imagining what it would be like to unpin it and run his fingers through it.

And then, inevitably, Dyson would say, "So what do you think, Elias?"

And he'd be caught flat-footed, dazed and confused, without a clue about what Dyson had just said. It had happened more than once.

Last Tuesday he had been watching Paul make one of his intricate charts on the whiteboard, which was not exactly fascinating. And his gaze had drifted over to Tallie and locked on the sight of her crossing her legs. The glimpse of smooth tanned thighs as she shifted was enough to make him lose track of all of Paul's lines and curves and squiggles.

"With me so far?" Paul asked, turning to face them.

Tallie had nodded, tapping the end of her pen against her front teeth, and Elias closed his eyes and squashed his errant thoughts and did his best to bully his brain cells into paying attention.

It was almost like being in high school again!

It made him furious. Though whether he was more furious with Tallie for being there or himself for being unable to ignore her was a question he didn't ever ask. So he challenged her, asked her tough, demanding questions.

And she gave him thoughtful, considered answers that showed she was paying attention, even if he wasn't. Further irritation.

"That Tallie's one sharp cookie," Dyson said to him one afternoon after a meeting in which she had once more pointed out things the rest of them hadn't seen.

Elias grunted. That was another thing. Cookies!

They were another part of the problem. She hadn't just brought them the first day. She brought them *every* day. Or if she didn't bring cookies, she brought strudels or cakes or tortes.

"Other offices have a candy dish," Elias grumbled. "We have a damned Viennese bakery."

"No one's complaining but you," Tallie pointed out unrepentantly.

Which was true, of course. But that didn't make it right. Or healthy! "They will when they get their cholesterol checked."

But instead of quitting, she offered to bring in fresh vegetables, too. And after that, she showed up every day with some baked delicacy and a tray of carrot and celery sticks, broccoli and cauliflower pieces and green and red pepper strips.

Elias didn't like it. "We don't have the budget for this sort of thing."

"The office isn't paying. It's my treat."

He muttered things about precedents, but she just smiled and kept on hauling the stuff in. And how was he supposed to forbid her to bring it in? She was the bloody president!

Of course, once the largesse began arriving regularly, everyone in the office seemed to materialize and stuff their faces.

And talk.

He'd never heard so much talking going on. He thought he'd always run a pretty easygoing office where people could speak their minds. But he'd never achieved the level of communication Tallie did with her damn cookies!

Ideas were exchanged. Thoughts were expressed. The staff didn't just talk about last night's Yankees game or how the Mets were doing or how Paul's wedding plans were going or what Lucy's grandchildren were doing. They talked about business, too. Sometimes reasonably good ideas actually emerged because of Tallie's cookies.

"Your old man is smarter than we thought." Dyson didn't know the whole story of how Tallie got to be president of Antonides Marine, but he did know that it was Aeolus's doing. He probably thought Aeolus picked her because she could bake. Little did he know.

Elias grunted. "Dumb luck."

"Could be," Dyson allowed with a grin. "But I'm not complaining." He leaned one hip on the edge of Elias's desk as he watched Tallie across the hall talking to Rosie. "She's good for this place. And she's one fine-looking woman."

Elias scowled. "You can't say that in the office."

"Tallie wouldn't care. She'd just tell me I was a fine-lookin' man." Dyson laughed in smug self-satisfaction.

Elias banged a drawer shut. "Which just shows how bad her taste is."

Dyson's grin broadened. He cocked his head. "You been a little grumpy ever since she got here. You jealous?"

Elias would have liked to have banged another drawer. "Not a chance. And we don't pay you to stand around spouting nonsense. Get to work."

"Just saying." Still chuckling, Dyson saluted and left.

"Shut the door," Elias called after him, and was glad when it banged shut, though he'd have preferred to do the slamming himself.

It was true what Dyson said. Tallie would probably say he was a fine-looking man. She joked with Dyson all the time. He even let her call him by his first name, Rufus, which absolutely no one else got away with. She laughed at his silly puns and corny jokes.

She spent hours with everyone on the staff discussing not just business matters, but their lives.

Elias would be sitting at his desk, trying to concentrate on work, and he'd hear Rosie nattering on about her boyfriend problems, and Tallie would be right there listening and clucking sympathetically. He'd be getting a cup of coffee so he could focus on the quarterly reports, and he'd overhear Dyson talking to her about old Jimmy Cliff movies and some girl named Sybella who was giving him a hard time. Or he'd go looking for Paul to discuss the information he was gathering about going back to using teak in their boats, and Paul would be in Tallie's office discussing wedding plans.

Hell, he hadn't even known Paul was getting married!

Tallie knew. She knew Paul's fiancée's name. She knew Lucy's grandchildren's names. She knew what Giulia had named the baby she'd finally had last Saturday.

"Giacomo," Tallie had told him, "after Vincent's father."

Elias didn't even know who Vincent was.

Tallie even knew the name of Cara's hair colourist.

"Why? Planning to color your hair pink?" Elias had asked her sarcastically when Cara had gone back to work.

Tallie had grinned. "Actually, I was making sure it wasn't anyone I let anywhere near my hair."

But that was the only time she'd grinned at him. Every other time she'd been business—all business.

And he had to admit that when she worked, she worked hard.

She came to work early and she left late. Because she spent damn near the whole workday listening to peoples' problems, Elias thought irritably.

But if he couldn't fault her diligence, he certainly didn't think much of her taste in men.

She was hanging around with Martin the Bore.

After pompous, irritating Martin had been the macho hotshot who'd carried her box of papers downstairs, he'd stopped by the office later that week to see if she was free for lunch.

"No, she's not," Elias said flatly before she could answer.

Tallie had looked at him, surprised.

"We have a lunch meeting."

"Really? I didn't know that." She looked at Martin and shrugged, smiling ruefully. "Sorry. I guess I can't."

"Dinner then?" Martin had lifted shaggy eyebrows hopefully.

Elias's jaw clenched. It was still clenched when Tallie turned to him, her look questioning.

"What?" he demanded.

She smiled guilelessly. "I just wondered if we might have a dinner meeting I don't know about, too?"

"No," he said curtly. "We don't."

"Fine." She turned away. "Then I'd love to go out with you," she said to Martin.

Elias, grinding his teeth, had turned and stalked away. But he knew she'd gone out with the Bore that night. He learned later she'd gone with him to the opera on the weekend.

"Opera?" Elias had choked on the word when she'd mentioned it on the following Monday morning

"Well, I prefer jazz," Tallie had said with a shrug. "But it was an educational experience. Martin knows a lot about opera."

"I'll bet," Elias had muttered, shaking his head. She really did have lousy taste in men.

Not that it mattered to him.

He was not—repeat, *not!*—interested in Tallie Savas. She was trouble, with a capital *T*. He was working with her because he had to. Just *working!* Nothing else.

But she was getting under his skin. He thought about her all the time. He hadn't thought about a woman this much since he'd been crazy in love with Millicent. And look what a disaster that had been, he reminded himself.

He put Tallie Savas firmly off-limits.

All the same, it was good he had the building renovations to work on. Tearing out walls became an excellent way to spend his evenings. It used up a lot of excess energy that his hormones would have preferred to spend another way. He hadn't ripped Martin the Bore's head off yet, either. And every night that Elias worked like a maniac, banging and slamming and ripping and hammering with Elvis Costello at full volume, he didn't hear the phone and didn't have to talk to his sisters or his father or his mother, either.

Hell, life was just about perfect.


Knowledge was power, wasn't it?

So if Tallie knew her father was setting her up and if she knew he hoped she would fall for Elias Antonides, all she had to do was resist.

Right?

Piece of cake.

In fact, that turned out to be the operative word. Or one of them, at least.

Cake. Cookies. Bread. Muffins. Scones. *Linzertorte. Gugelhupf. Striezel. Buchtel. Powidlkolatschen. Semmel. Vanillekipferln,* courtesy of her Viennese baker friend, Klaus. And *baklava, ravani, koulourakia and megthalpeta,* courtesy of her mother.

You name it, Tallie baked it.

Every night when she got home from the office, she fed Harvey, fixed her own dinner, did her Pilates to relieve stress. And then she went into the kitchen and got out the flour and sugar and butter and spices and undid all the work Pilates had done—because baking was how she really relieved stress.

And Tallie was stressed.

Or maybe, she thought grimly, she was frustrated.

Who wouldn't be if they had to spend days looking at—and not touching—as fine a specimen of the male of the species as Elias Antonides?

Well, she supposed Dyson and Paul weren't.

And Rosie had a boyfriend, and Lucy had a husband, and Trina and Cara drooled over boy bands and one of the new young Latin ballplayers on the New York Mets. None of them even seemed to notice that Elias Antonides simply oozed sex appeal.

Lucky them.

Unfortunately Tallie noticed. She noticed the way Elias had of furrowing his brow when he was deep in thought. She noticed the dimple in his cheek that flashed when he grinned. She sat in the meetings, and while she was supposed to be listening, she was noticing what large capable hands Elias had and that he had calluses on his fingers which no man who pushed a pen all day should have.

More than she wanted to, Tallie noticed muscles flexing beneath his shirt that he hadn't got from pushing any pen, either. There was not much about Elias Antonides that she didn't notice, more's the pity.

Worse, he challenged her. He was constantly staring at her as if he wished she would just disappear. And then he'd ask some pointed question or wait until Paul had outlined some particularly boring facts, and then Elias would look at her and say, "And what do you think, Ms Savas?"

After being caught out the first time and blushing bright red, then having to make up something on the spot that, fortunately, wasn't too far off base because she'd done a lot of reading the night before, she had vowed never to be caught again.

It was almost a game to her now—watching him surreptitiously, waiting for him to pounce with his question, then answering him with all the wisdom and forethought she could muster.

She began to look forward to it, determined to pick up on things he might not have noticed, to show him she was good at what she did, too.

Some days after a meeting she felt like she'd been in a sparring match with the two of them, challenging and feeding off each other. Elias Antonides got her adrenaline flowing.

And that was even scarier.

Brian used to get her adrenaline flowing. Lieutenant Brian O'Malley had been the last man Tallie would have imagined she'd fall for. But he'd always had a way of challenging her, of making her think about things differently, of making her mad and then of making her laugh.

He had loved her for herself, not the companies her father owned. He had helped her find the best part of herself. When his plane had crashed on a training exercise seven months before their wedding, a part of Tallie had died with him. No one had ever made her feel as alive as Brian had.

Until now.

Not that Elias was anything like Brian!

He wasn't. Was…not. Period.

He was handsome—far handsomer than her tough, redheaded, freckle-faced Brian. He was smooth and arrogant, which Brian had never been. Besides, Elias was her father's choice, not hers. And if he sparred with her, it was because he was stuck with her for the next two years.

It was not an ideal situation.

She came home tired but edgy, running whatever Elias had said that day over in her mind, thinking about how she might have answered him better, sharper, quicker. Almost always she could think of something.

At the time, though, she was often distracted by the physical Elias Antonides as much as the sharp-as-a-whip managing director. Hormones that had been dormant since Brian's death.

It was disconcerting, to say the least.

It was particularly disconcerting to have it happen at work. Nothing—not even Brian—had distracted her from her work before. Of course Brian had never been where she'd worked. But Elias was. And Elias did.

She'd even found herself fantasizing about what he looked

like without his oxford cloth shirts and his well-pressed khakis. She wondered what he looked like *naked!*

So she baked. Furiously. And she went out with Martin.

She never fantasized about Martin.

He wasn't bad looking. He was actually reasonably nice looking in a pigeon-chested, pinch-lipped sort of way. He had an engaging grin when it could be teased out of him. And he had very nice hazel eyes. She liked his eyes. But had she thought about him naked?

No. Never.

He looked as if he could use a square meal, but he never ate one. He ate a lot of macrobiotic things like brown rice and bulgar with bean sprouts. It was healthy, he told her. He didn't think her baking was healthy at all, but he went out with her anyway.

"To convince me of the error of my ways," she told Harvey.

Martin, she discovered early on, could pontificate on any topic—and did. At length. He was interesting in a long-winded sort of way. His favorite topic was his view of the world and how it was failing to live up to his standards.

Tallie herself was in danger of not living up to them, too, because the night he took her to the opera she very nearly fell asleep.

She should have stayed home and gone over the material Elias had given her—her "homework" for the weekend. But she'd spent most of the day on Saturday doing just that—and found herself distracted with thoughts of the way Elias had looked holding Giulia's baby when she'd brought him into the office to show him off the day before.

It hadn't been Elias's idea. The women had been passing Giacomo around, cooing and gooing over him. Trina had been holding him when Elias stuck his head out of his office and wondered sarcastically when they had started providing child care and when Trina was going to finish typing up the material he'd given her that morning.

Tallie would have said something pithy and sarcastic right back. But Trina, in her haste to do the right thing, actually did something better.

"Oh, gosh, right now," she'd said—and thrust the baby into Elias's arms as she'd darted back to the steno office to get to work.

Tallie didn't know who looked more shocked, Elias or the baby. She'd thought he would hand Giacomo straight back to his mother.

But he didn't. After a moment's stunned silence, he'd shifted the baby awkwardly until he had it settled more comfortably in his arms, and then they regarded each other solemnly.

And then he'd smiled.

*Elias* had smiled—not the baby!

It was the most amazing thing. She could close her eyes and still see the tender look on his face. There was no impatience, no irritation. None of the things he most commonly aimed at her.

And that was when she'd realized it hadn't been a good thing Trina had done at all, because it had the unfortunate effect of making him even more appealing than he usually was—and in a different way.

It had been reasonably easy to resist a man who was simply physically attractive. It was a lot harder to ignore her attraction when she saw him with a baby.

He also listened patiently to phone calls from his sisters or requests from his mother. For all of Elias's hard-nosed attitude in business, he was, Tallie had realized after being there just a few days, a soft touch when it came to his family.

Of course, he had to be, or he'd never have stayed on as managing director of Antonides Marine. But it wasn't just his faimly. That same afternoon, after Giulia left, Tallie caught him on the phone agreeing to buy cookie dough from some school fundraiser for one of his mother's friends' granddaughters.

Then he'd noticed her listening and had scowled fiercely at her.

Tallie had grinned. It was like verifying the Big Bad Wolf liked sentimental old movies.

But it was also worrisome. And it had made her say yes when Martin wanted her to go with him to some totally boring lecture at Cooper Union on global warming.

* * *

His mother had stopped trying to set him up with women.

Used to her perennial efforts to get herself a new daughter-in-law, Elias was at first relieved by the sudden lack of women being shoved down his throat.

And then he realized why.

His mother didn't have to find him a suitable wife because she thought his father already had. And Elias couldn't keep saying, as he'd said to all her earlier efforts, "No, Mom. No, I'm not interested. No. No. No."

Because if he did, they'd know she was getting to him.

He knew what he needed to do. He needed to find his own woman.

Not to marry, God forbid. He was adamant about that. But to go out with, to flirt with, to charm and tease and have sex with.

Man did not live by work alone, as his father was often inclined to tell him.

Elias knew that. He'd had Gretl, hadn't he?

But it had been months since he'd had Gretl or any other woman. Obviously he needed to find one—a recreational partner—not a life mate.

And definitely not the president of Antonides Marine!

So on Monday he went out after work instead of heading down to the second floor where he was knocking out the walls of one of the offices . There was a bar called Casey's down the block, and he dropped in and had a beer and studied the unattached women at the bar.

The noise was appalling. The women, when he talked to them, were brainless. And none of them had hair that made him want to run his fingers through it. So he finished his beer and went back and knocked down another wall.

Tuesday he tried a different place—a club that had a jazz quartet. He liked jazz and he thought he might meet a more kindred spirit. He did not think about the woman in his office who liked jazz but went to see an opera with Martin the Bore.

There was a girl called Abigail at the jazz place. She hit on him and he didn't resist. He spent the evening listening to her talk about her crazy roommates and her annoying mother and he wondered if Tallie played jazz CDs while she was baking. Abigail gave him her phone number. He discovered later he'd left it on the bar and he didn't even care.

Wednesday evening he went to the local health club. Ordinarily he played basketball when he went. But there were no women on his basketball team. So instead he played racquetball with a French teacher called Clarice from Bordeaux.

They played hard, and she looked pretty enticing sweaty, and he thought that was promising, so he invited her out for a meal after.

She shook her head, batted her lashes, held out her hand and purred, "Let's go to my place instead."

God knew what would have happened at Clarice's place—and Elias did, too—if he had got there.

But as they left the health club and were walking toward Clarice's flat, his mother rang him on his cell phone. "I should take it," he told Clarice. She could think it was business. And the truth was, if he didn't take it, his mother would just call back at an even less opportune time.

"Have you heard from Martha?" Helena demanded.

"Nope. Not a word." Which wasn't exactly a disappointment. Elias heard from all his family far too often, as far as he was concerned.

"She just broke up with Julian," his mother went on, her voice rising. "She's very upset."

"She'll get over it," Elias said wearily. He shot Clarice an apologetic glance. "She's a big girl." Besides, his own disastrous marriage didn't qualify him to solve anybody's relationship problems. "I've got to go."

But Helena wasn't going to be easily dismissed. "You've got to talk to her, Elias. Calm her down. She listens to you."

Then she was the only one, Elias thought. "She'll work it out, Ma. She'll be fine."

"I don't think so. You know Martha."

Yes, he did. He knew all the hysterical members of his family who thought the world revolved around them. "Ma, I have to go."

But it was too late. He could already see Clarice withdrawing. Whether it was the "Ma" that did it (what woman wanted to take a man home who spent the walk there listening to his mother?) or something else, Elias didn't know. But by the time he managed to shut his mother up, Clarice was remembering she'd promised to play canasta with her elderly neighbor tonight.

"She's a real card shark. And lonely. I shouldn't disappoint her," Clarice was smiling and backing away.

Elias could take a hint. "Some other time, then."

"Of course," Clarice agreed.

But not Thursday. Because all day Thursday Elias was at Tom Corbett's factory with Paul and Tallie, making notes, talking to Corbett and his production manager, getting a hands-on feel for the place.

While he asked question after question and Paul went over the books and charts, Tallie just wandered around, chatted with the employees, poked her nose in this and that and smiled.

She'd brought along some sort of star-shaped cookies that smelled of cinnamon for Corbett and his minions, and the next thing Elias knew she was trading recipes with one of the shipping clerks.

"She's the president?" Corbett said doubtfully. He also seemed to be appreciating Tallie's figure a little more than Elias thought was entirely necessary.

"She is," he said sharply.

"Don't know how you keep your mind on business," Corbett said frankly. "Or your hands off her."

It was one of those totally politically incorrect things that no one these days was supposed to say. It was also unfortunately and annoyingly true.

Tallie Savas was tempting the hell out of him.

And every day it was getting worse.

# CHAPTER FOUR

SHE WASN'T there.

Here it was, ten past ten Friday morning—ten past the time he and Paul and Dyson and Ms President of Antonides Marine were supposed to be having their meeting about the Corbett's acquisition—and she hadn't stuck her nose in the door!

Hadn't bothered to call, either.

How responsible was that?

Of course, Elias reminded himself, he shouldn't be surprised. When his father had first sprung Tallie-Savas-is-our-new-president on him, he had been sure it wouldn't last. He'd thought she'd treat it as a lark, a game rich girls played.

The way she'd acted for the past three weeks, though, had made Elias wonder if he'd been wrong. During that time Tallie had given every indication of taking the job seriously.

Still, she hadn't asked Corbett any questions yesterday. She'd wandered off, poked around, hadn't focused on any of the really important issues he and Corbett and Paul had discussed.

She hadn't said anything much on the way back in the car, either. And every time he'd slanted her a glance, she'd turned her gaze out the window. Bored, he supposed now.

And this morning she simply hadn't bothered to show up!

As he had come in prepared to steel himself against whatever enticing baked delicacy she would bring, not to mention what skirt she would be wearing that would show off her lovely long legs, he felt unaccountably annoyed. The least she could have done was call.

But she'd done nothing. There had been no whiff of cinnamon, no hint of cardamom or apple when he pushed open the door. There had been no cheery good-morning to Rosie, no request for a play-by-play on the latest of Paul's wedding plans. Nothing.

Because she didn't appear.

Everyone else did. Dyson, Paul, Rosie, Lucy and all the temp girls all stuck their heads into his office to ask where she was.

"How would I know?" Elias replied irritably.

"Haven't you heard from her?"

"Not a word."

He didn't know where she was. He didn't *care* where she was, he told himself firmly. He set down his pen, leaned back in his chair and took a deep breath, the first he'd taken since his father had sprung the awful news on him, and felt lighter.

Emptier.

Emptier?

Nonsense. He had just grown used to the continual buzz Tallie created in the office. It was a relief not to have her stirring things up. It would just take a little readjustment. That was all.

The phone rang, and for once he hoped it was his father so he could tell the old man that the president of Antonides Marine hadn't bothered to show up.

But the gruff male voice that boomed in his ear said, "Savas here."

Elias straightened in his chair. "Yes, Mr. Savas," he said crisply to Tallie's father. "What can I do for you?"

"Put my daughter on the phone."

Elias frowned. "I beg your pardon."

"I want to talk to Thalia." Pause. "She's not answering her cell phone because she knows it's me."

Elias's brows lifted. "Why?" he couldn't help asking.

"Because you've told her to, I would guess," Socrates retorted.

Because *he* had told he to? Elias's mind boggled.

"Blasted girl," Socrates went on. "Won't say a word."

A word about what? Elias wondered.

Socrates told him. "Goes on and on about what doesn't matter. This architect with dreadlocks and some girl with blue hair. But about the business—nothing! And you—" There was another abrupt pause. Then "What do you think of my daughter?"

Um. Er. "She's…very sharp."

"Of course she is sharp. She's a Savas! Beautiful, too, don't you think?"

"She's a beautiful woman," Elias agreed with as much dispassionate indifference as he could manage. She was drop-dead gorgeous, but he wasn't going to say that to her old man.

"That's what I tell her. So why does she want only to be a businessman? She is a *woman!* One hundred percent woman! A woman like my Thalia should be married, should have children. She will make a good wife and mother someday, yes?"

Visions of Tallie Savas with little weedy, floppy-haired Martins flickered across Elias's brain. He took a death grip on the receiver. "If she wants. Who knows?" he said casually.

"I know!" Clearly Socrates had his mind made up.

Elias felt a momentary pang of sympathy for Tallie Savas. Her father was as bad as his mother.

"And when she is married I will not be worrying about her, wondering where she is," Socrates went on. "That will be her husband's job. You tell her to call me." It was an order, not a suggestion.

"I'll give her the message."

Elias could just imagine what Tallie would say to him delivering a message from her old man. In fact the thought made him smile and shove back his chair. He went out into the reception area, glad he had an excuse to find out where the hell she was.

"Call Ms Savas," he instructed Rosie. "Tell her she's late."

While he stood there tapping his foot, Rosie rang Tallie's home phone and her cell phone. Apparently she wasn't answering his calls, either.

"Do you suppose she's sick?" Paul asked.

"She'd be home in bed if she were sick, wouldn't she?" Elias snapped. "I'm sure she's just got better things to do."

"Like what?" Paul looked bewildered.

"How the hell should I know? We're not waiting." Elias turned and stalked into the boardroom. "We had a meeting scheduled. She knew it. If she can't be bothered, that's her problem. Come on."

Obediently, but worriedly, Dyson and Paul followed.

The meeting went as all pre-Tallie meetings had gone. One of them, in this case Dyson, acted as the disinterested bystander. He had done no research on Corbett's. He had nothing to gain, nothing to lose. He was there to observe, to ask questions, to pull things together. Paul was there to discuss the financial issues, the market, the reasons for buying Corbett's from his standpoint, and the reasons against. And Elias was there to run through what he had discovered from talking to Corbett, to lay out all the pros and cons from the broader scope of the company.

They'd done it before—lots of times.

It should have been second nature. It was, really, Elias assured himself. It was just that they'd got used to Tallie saying, "Yes, but what about kids?" Or, "Have you considered that women don't always want to go out and sail around in boats in the freezing cold and get wet?"

Stuff that, frankly, they hadn't considered.

There were odd, awkward pauses, now and then, that made it feel to Elias as if they were actually waiting for her input.

And then the door cracked open.

All three of them looked up.

Something silver poked its way through the door. There was a thump and a bonk and a female mutter of annoyance. Suddenly Rosie was pushing the door wide-open and saying, "Here. For heaven's sake, let me get that! What happened? What are you doing here?"

"I work here!" It was Tallie's voice, defiant and determined and—

What the hell?

They all stared, astonished, as Tallie, leaning heavily on a pair of crutches, thumped her way into the room. There was an instant's total shock. Then all three men leaped to their feet.

Dyson pulled out a chair for her. "Here. Sit."

Paul said, "Let me," and eased her into it.

Elias contented himself with looming over her, demanding, "What the hell happened to you?"

She was a mess. She was tattered and disheveled, her face was flushed and there was a scrape on her cheek, her normally ruthlessly tamed hair was poking out from its pins, her legs were bare of pantyhose, both had skinned knees, and her lower left leg was in a bright-purple cast the ended just below the knee.

Tallie smiled ruefully. "I got run over by a truck."

Elias gaped at her. *"You what?"*

She laughed a little painfully and shifted carefully into the chair that Paul had helped her to. "Well, not really run over. Just knocked down, really. I was crossing the street and some guy was turning and—" she shrugged "—he didn't seem to notice I was in the crosswalk."

"Good God!" Elias wasn't sure if it was a prayer or a cry of exasperation. "Didn't you notice *him,* for Christ's sake? You could have been killed!"

"Well, I wasn't." She gave him a bright smile that was way too ragged around the edges for Elias's satisfaction. "Fortunately," she added reflectively after a moment, "or not. I suppose it depends on your point of view. You probably wish he'd done a better job of it."

"Don't be an ass," Elias snapped. He was furious now, though he wasn't sure at whom. He snapped his pencil in half and stalked up and down the length of the room. "What the hell are you doing here? Why aren't you in the hospital?"

"Don't yell." Tallie winced. "And stop pacing. It gives me a headache."

He stopped and spun around. "Are you concussed? Did you hit your head? Your cheek is cut," he noticed. Quickly he crouched down beside her to get a better look and discovered her big brown eyes just inches from his own. Abruptly he stood up. "Why aren't you in the hospital?"

It was all he could do to moderate his tone. He wanted to strangle someone. Preferably the guy with the truck.

"Because," Tallie said levelly, "they don't keep people in hospitals these days. They patch them up and send them home.

And—" she held up a hand and forestalled his next question before he could even get it out of his mouth "—there was no point in sitting home when I can sit here just as well. It's only a broken ankle. And a few bumps and bruises." She shifted in her chair and winced, then managed another smile. "No big deal."

Elias stared. So did Paul and Dyson.

"You could have been killed, you idiot woman!" he yelled.

"I realize that," Tallie said quietly, and there was the slightest quaver in her voice. "But I wasn't. So obviously I've been spared for a purpose—" she offered Elias a faint grin "—like making your life hell?"

Elias snorted and raked a hand through his hair. He cracked his knuckles and picked up another pencil and began pacing again. How could she expect he'd just stand still? "I can deal with you," he muttered. Or he would be able to if she'd stop doing such stupid things and go home and rest or file her nails or bake her damn cookies or—

He snapped the pencil in half.

"It'll be okay. Really." Now she sounded as if she was soothing him! "I'm all right. I've broken my ankle before. I'm an old hand at it actually. Done it three times now. The bad thing in this instance," she said sadly, "is that my cinnamon rolls and bear claws all landed in the gutter."

"That's the bad thing, is it?" Elias still wanted to throttle her. "No one needs your damned cinnamon rolls!"

"I'll bet they were good," Dyson said with a grin.

Tallie ignored Elias and smiled back at Dyson. "I'll make some more," she promised.

"Excellent!"

"That'll be great!" Paul was beaming now, all eagerness, too.

Didn't the idiot notice the cuts on her hands? The cast on her leg? Elias ground his teeth. "She's hurt. She isn't going to be making cinnamon rolls!"

"Well, I didn't mean right away," Paul said hastily. "I just meant, when she's feeling better—"

"When I'm feeling better, I'll make more," Tallie reiterated. Then she turned to Elias. "Don't make faces."

He barred his teeth at her. "Why? Does that give you a head-ache, too?"

"Actually, it does. Look, could we just go on with the meet-ing? I'm sorry I'm late. I was—"

"Hit by a truck," Elias snarled before she could say it again. "Have you called your father?"

"Of course not!" Tallie looked as if the idea had never oc-curred to her.

"He doesn't know?"

"No one knows. Well, except the staff at the emergency room, the EMTs and you guys. I didn't take out an ad in the *Times!* Or call my folks. Frankly, my father is the last person I'd tell. He'd fuss."

"He already has. He rang this morning."

The little colour in her cheeks seemed to fade completely. Elias thought she might faint. "He called here?"

"Looking for you. Worrying about you. Said you were avoid-ing him." It had been more satisfying when he'd thought she had been avoiding Socrates. But maybe she had, even before the truck incident. "Don't call if you don't want to," Elias said. "I've dealt with him."

"You have?" She looked stricken.

"Yes, so don't worry about him.  Come on," he said. "You need to go home."

"I'm *not* going home. I came to work to attend this damn meeting, and I'm going to do it."

"Afraid I'll do something you wouldn't approve of?" he chal-lenged her.

She met his gaze. "Afraid you won't think I'm holding up my end of the deal," Tallie replied.

Which was exactly what he had thought. Elias ground his teeth, then shrugged. "Fine. Be stupid."  He turned his gaze to Paul. "Keep going. If Ms Savas wants to be a pigheaded, obsti-nate idiot, that's entirely her affair."

Paul didn't seem to remember where he was. "Um, let's see—" He fumbled with his notes, punched a couple of keys on his computer to see where he was in the presentation. "I'm not sure— I don't—" He looked around helplessly.

"The waterproof-clothing line," Elias prompted.

"Oh, er, right." Paul found the spot in his notes and the right material on the screen. Squaring his shoulders and sparing one more worried glance at Tallie, he launched into his report once more.

Elias didn't listen.

Stupid, stupid woman. What the hell did she think she was doing coming to work after she'd nearly been killed? He couldn't take his eyes off her as Paul droned on. He knew he should be paying attention. It was important.

But he couldn't. He sat watching Tallie while Paul's words flowed over him like water over a rock, but with less effect.

Tallie, of course, sat straight in her chair, pen in hand, notebook on her lap, purple-casted leg and foot stuck out in front of her. Her gaze was fixed on Paul and she was listening intently. Probably hanging on his every word, Elias thought irritably. She even made notes.

But now and then he saw her wince or grimace, then shift in her chair as if trying to find a comfortable spot. The only spot she was likely to be comfortable in was her bed. She had to be in pain. A sane woman would have left the hospital and gone straight home.

He waited for her to smile gamely and call it quits. She never did. She sat still and breathed carefully, shallowly and every now and then ran her tongue along her upper lip.

What the hell was she trying to prove?

Well, actually he knew what she was trying to prove. She was trying to prove herself to her father, who didn't think she ought to be in the business world at all.

And—Elias flexed his shoulders guiltily here—he knew she was also trying to prove herself to him. He'd made things hard on her over the past few weeks. He'd challenged her, doubted her, pushed her.

And she had responded with determination. She had done the job.

She didn't need to sit here turning white around the mouth, a sheen of perspiration on her forehead.

Abruptly Elias stood up. "Okay, that's it. I need a little more time to digest this. Thanks, Paul. We'll finish up on Monday," he said to his shocked assistant. Then he turned to Tallie, "Come on, Prez, we're going home."

It took a second for Tallie to even react, which, as far as Elias was concerned, just proved his point.

Then her brow furrowed and, naturally, she objected. "What? What are you talking about?"

"Time to close the shop." He was flicking down the blinds in the windows and opening the door to the reception area as he spoke. "We're ending the meeting. Heading out. It's Friday. We close early on Fridays in the summer."

"Since when?"

"Since now," Elias said in a tone that brooked no argument. He fixed a glare on Dyson and Paul that dared them to dispute it.

Dyson grinned broadly and rubbed his hands. "That's right! I nearly forgot. I'm outa here!"

Paul, still looking a little dazed, was fumbling with his notes. "Uh, yeah, but—"

"But *I'm* the president," Tallie protested.

"And you can be president from your house just as well." Elias stood by her chair and held out a hand. "Let's go."

She looked at it but didn't put hers in it. Figured. Stubborn woman.

"Tallie." Elias tapped his foot impatiently.

Sighing, she finally took his hand and he helped her to her feet. But when she tugged her hand to get free, he didn't go away. He fitted her crutches under her arms and held the door for her.

"But I'm not leaving," Tallie said "I'm having lunch with Martin."

"Like hell!"

"I am," Tallie insisted, trying to maneuver the corner on her crutches. But the effects of the accident finally seemed to be taking their toll. She was wobblier now than when she'd come in. She teetered and would have fallen if Elias hadn't caught her.

Whoa.

Tallie Tough-As-Nails Savas was incredibly soft. Round. Delectable. Her father's words echoed in Elias's head: *One hundred percent woman.*

Oh, yes.

"Steady now," he said gruffly, shifting her away from him, turning his head so he would stop breathing in the soft citrus scent of her shampoo.

"I am steady," she muttered, her knuckles white as she gripped the hand bars on the crutches.

"Sure you are." He steered her carefully out the meeting room door and into the main office. Rosie and Dyson and Paul and the temp girls all looked on nervously.

"What are you looking at? Don't you have work to do?" Elias demanded.

They all shook their heads.

"They were just leaving," Tallie said impishly. "Weren't you?"

"On our way," Dyson agreed. But not one moved, watching rapt as Tallie and Elias lurched through the office, like a stumbling man in a three-legged race. This was never going to work.

"Here," Elias said to Dyson. And in one swift movement he slipped Tallie's crutches out from under her arms, thrust them at Dyson, then scooped the president of Antonides Marine into his arms and headed for the door.

"What do you think you're doing?" she demanded furiously.

Elias kicked the door open. "Taking you home."

"Martin—"

"Can bore somebody else," he said as Paul held the door for him to go out and down the hall.

"Elias, stop!" Tallie wriggled in his arms, giving him some very interesting tactile sensations that did nothing to make him want to let her go. Then suddenly she sucked in a sharp breath and stopped.

"What's wrong? Does it hurt?" he demanded, staring down into the dark-brown eyes only inches from his.

She swallowed. Their gazes were still locked. "If I say yes will you put me down?"

"Not a chance."

She made a face. "I feel like an idiot," she muttered as he carried her toward the elevator.

"Because you are," Elias said flatly. "You broke your leg, you stupid woman. You should never have come in at all. You should have gone home!" The elevator door opened and he stepped inside. Paul followed with the crutches.

"I broke my *ankle*," Tallie corrected. "It's not a big deal. It hurts, yes. It's swollen, yes. But I'm not going to die from it. Besides, if I'd gone home you'd have thought I was shirking my duty."

He glared at her.

She gave him a saccharine smiled in return. Then she resolutely turned her head away from him again, as if not looking at him would allow her to believe she wasn't being cradled in his arms.

Well, she might be able to deny it, but Elias couldn't. She was too solid, too soft, too *real* to deny. And when she turned her head he got another noseful of soft curly hair. He held his breath.

The elevator bumped and the door opened. Paul sprinted ahead. "I'll flag down a taxi." He shot out the door just as Martin de Boer was coming in.

"Tallie!" De Boer, looking windblown and very journalist-about-town with his leather briefcase and his bomber jacket, stared, horrified.

"Oh, Martin! Hi. I broke my ankle. About lunch today—"

"She won't be able to make it," Elias said, shouldering past Martin and out onto the sidewalk.

"Wait!" Tallie elbowed him sharply in the ribs and craned her neck to look back. "I need to talk to Martin."

"Phone him."

But there was no need because de Boer had come after them. "My God, Tallie. What happened?"

"I had a small accident." She was wriggling around, trying to see de Boer over his shoulder.

"She got hit by a truck," Elias said flatly. "Hold still, damn it," he snapped at her, for which he got another elbow.

"Dear God." De Boer looked appalled.

"I'm fine," Tallie said.

"She could have been killed, of course," Elias added conversationally.

"But I wasn't!"

De Boer, whose eyes went from one to the other as if he were watching a tennis match, didn't seem capable of saying anything at all.

"I was going to call you, Martin," Tallie said earnestly. "To let you know that I probably shouldn't go out—"

"Sanity rears its head at last," Elias muttered.

"But," Tallie went on forcefully, ignoring his comment, "if you want, we could eat at my place."

Sanity obviously didn't last.

Elias didn't even give de Boer a chance to respond to that idiotic suggestion. He headed for the curb where Paul had flagged down a taxi.

De Boer tagged along like a junkyard dog, patting Tallie's arm awkwardly. "Well, thank you, but, er, I don't think so." He gave her his hopeless grin. "All things considered, I think we should reschedule. Is she really all right?" he asked Elias doubtfully. "Did she fall on her head?"

"I'm fine!" Tallie insisted as Elias lowered her into the back seat.

"She's fine," Elias echoed, deadpan, "as you can see."

De Boer looked from Tallie in the cab to Elias, taking the crutches from Paul and climbing in beside her, and backed away. "Well, it, um, looks as if things are under control," he said to Tallie. "I'll give you a call."

"They're not—"

But Elias slammed the door shut.

"Where to?" the driver asked.

Elias looked at Tallie to give her address. She glared mutinously back at him. He looked at the driver and shrugged.

The driver rolled his eyes. "Ain't got all day, folks."

Tallie's jaw tightened, but finally she muttered her address and the taxi shot away.

Tallie's apartment was only about half a dozen blocks away. Elias was surprised at that. He'd pegged her as a hotshot, fast-track Upper-West-Sider. So she was walking to work and got hit? Where? he wondered, studying the street corners as they passed.

Tallie was looking out the window, determinedly ignoring

him. Probably wishing he'd let bloody de Boer bring her home, he thought irritably.

She didn't say a word until they were on her block. Then she leaned forward and said to the driver, "This one," and gestured to a four-story brick building right on the East River's edge. Like many of the buildings in the neighborhood—including the one that housed Antonides Marine International—this one was a converted warehouse, home to a funky used-clothing store, a kitchenwares shop, a music store and a pizza place on the ground floor with three stories of loft apartments and businesses above. Elias paid the taxi and climbed out, then reached back to get the crutches, but Tallie already had them.

"I can manage," she said, a mulish look on her face.

"You'll fall on your face." She was as pale as a ghost. "Don't be ridiculous. Just give me the crutches and—"

She gave him the crutches—one of them—right where he least expected it. Or wanted it!

"God almighty!"

Elias jumped back and nearly doubled over. Good thing she hadn't put any force behind it. If she had, she'd have settled his mother's "isn't it about time you got me some grandchildren" issue once and for all. And not in the way his mother would have preferred.

Not the way *he* would prefer, either. "Bloody hell!" He gritted his teeth and waited for the pain to subside.

"Sorry." Tallie's cheeks flushed. "Are you…all right?"

"No, damn it. I'm not all right," Elias said through his teeth. "You fight dirty, Prez."

She had the grace to look ashamed, but then she lifted her chin and said haughtily, "Well, if you'd get out of my way—"

When Elias could move again, he did just that. "Fine. Do it yourself. Be my guest." He stood back watching as she wriggled and squirmed and eventually made her way out of the back seat of the taxi one slow, painful inch at a time.

The taxi driver, waiting, shot Elias despairing looks and tapped his fingers impatiently on the steering wheel.

Elias just shrugged.

"You ain't no gentleman," the driver told him.

"And she's no lady."

The cab driver who had seen her jab with the crutch barked a laugh. "Ain't that the truth!"

Tallie glowered at them both. Then she concentrated on extricating herself from the taxi and negotiating the curb. Elias let her do it. Then he slammed the door shut and the cab sped away.

"Now you'll just have to flag down another one," Tallie pointed out.

Elias ignored her. He crossed the sidewalk to the door of her building, then turned and wordlessly held out his hand for her key.

The look she gave him promised a fight. But apparently the logistics of dealing with the door and the key and the crutches were—for the moment—more than she wanted to deal with.

With a long-suffering sigh, Tallie handed over the key.

Elias opened the door, held it for her, got a muttered ungracious "Thank you" for his trouble. Then he followed her into the building.

The foyer was utilitarian. Brick and steel, clean and spare, with a door to the stairs and an elevator at the far end. Tallie turned and gave him a level but annoyed look.

"Okay. I'm here. You've seen me to the door. Mission accomplished. Thank you again. I'll see you on Monday."

"Not a chance." Elias stepped around her and headed for the elevator, leaving her behind. He pushed the button and waited while it whirred to life overhead and begin its descent.

Tallie glared at him. "You're a pain in the ass, Antonides."

"So I've been told."

She looked longingly toward the door that said Stairs on it.

*Go for it, sweetheart,* Elias thought irritably. *See how far you get.* He turned back to the elevator.

A full thirty seconds passed before her crutches thumped his way across the tile. She reached him just as the door of the elevator opened. He held it open silently. Tallie hobbled past him and gave him a fulminating glare on her way in.

Elias stepped in after her. "Would've been a hike," he said conversationally.

She pressed the button marked three. "I would have loved to do it just to spite you," she admitted, surprising him. Then she shrugged. "But when I thought about what would happen if I fainted halfway up…" She gave him a wry, weary grin. A ghost of a smile, really.

"You wouldn't faint," he said, and somehow believed it was true. She was tough, was Tallie Savas. He might fight her, but he respected her. Looking at her now, he saw that she was white around the mouth again and there was really very little colour left in her cheeks at all.

"Are you okay?" he asked warily, discovering that he much preferred the spitfire Ms Savas to the one who looked as if she were in danger of keeling over.

"Yes, of course," she said with some asperity. "I didn't take the stairs because I know my limits."

He grinned his relief. "That's my girl."

"I am *not* your girl!"

Which was exactly what he knew she'd say, which was exactly why he'd said it. His grin broadened.

The elevator shuddered to a halt and the door slid open. They stepped out into a small vestibule painted a bright poppy red. There were three doors besides the elevator. Tallie nodded at the purple door opposite it.

"That's mine," she said and, bowing to the inevitable, waited while he unlocked it and pushed it open. She went in, then turned back to offer him a real, if wan, smile this time. "Now I really am home, and I didn't faint, and while it wasn't necessary for you to accompany me, I suppose I should appreciate it."

"I suppose you should," he said. "And I'm sure you *won't* appreciate this, Prez, but I'm not leaving."

# CHAPTER FIVE

WHAT was she supposed to do? Throw herself in front of him and stop him?

Tallie had done enough throwing of herself for one day, thank you very much, even if the throwing hadn't been her idea.

She *hurt*, damn it.

Her ankle was throbbing, her head ached, the scrapes on her hands and arm were stiff and smarting. It felt like rigor mortis setting in.

But she had sucked it up and gone to the office—had never considered *not* going in to work today. As long as she was alive and breathing—and unhospitalized—she had been determined to go to work, to prove to Mr. All-Work-and-No-Play Antonides that her level of commitment to the job equaled his.

But a woman's strength and stamina and grit only went so far. And then she was done. Shot. Kaput.

Tallie was kaput. It was true what she'd said in the elevator. She might have fainted had she tried the stairs—and God knew she'd *wanted* to take the stairs and prove herself independent and whole!

But she was feeling less independent and whole by the minute. And right now if she didn't sit down soon she was going to fall down and she knew it.

After having been carried—*carried!*—through the streets of New York (well, thank God, actually only Brooklyn) and in front of Martin (who had been shot at by terrorists and made it sound like a walk in the park) Tallie didn't think she could stand further humiliation today. Not and survive.

So she just looked at Elias's straight back as he walked past her into her living room and did the only thing she could—she stuck out her tongue.

Then she turned ever so carefully on her crutches because, even though she'd used crutches plenty of times before and knew it was a skill that would come back quickly, she wasn't swift on them at the moment. She was decidedly shaky. Her arms, unaccustomed to bearing her weight, were fatigued. The scrapes she'd sustained were stinging. And her ankle, which the doc had said to rest, elevate and use ice on, was now throbbing beyond belief.

He had given her painkillers. But she had adamantly refused any at the hospital. She'd been determined to have all her wits about her in the meeting. Now her wits seemed expendable. Where was that bottle of pills?

"Where's my briefcase?" She looked around, but didn't see it.

Elias was looking around her apartment, probably making more judgments about her competence based on the fact that she furnished from thrift shops and the Goodwill. At least he didn't seem offended that Harvey was walking around him, sniffing, checking him out.

"Where is it?" she demanded again, feeling a little panicky now. "Elias?"

"Oh, give it a rest. You're not going to work now." He had stopped staring around the apartment and was looking straight at her. His hands were jammed into the pockets of his khakis, which had the effect of making him look very masculine and gunfighterish.

The last thing Tallie needed was a gunfighter. Unless he could shoot her and put her out of her misery.

She took a breath. "I know I'm not going to work," she said with all the patience she could muster. "I just need my briefcase. My pain pills are in it."

"Then why the hell didn't you say so? It's at the office. I'll call Rosie. She can bring it over." Elias dug his mobile phone out of his pocket and punched in a number, then waited, tapping his foot, looking at Tallie for signs that she might explode before his eyes.

She tried to look more patient than she felt.

There was apparently no answer because Elias continued to wait. He tapped. Waited some more. Muttered to himself about bloody answering machines, then punched in the number again and waited some more, until finally in disgust he flicked the phone off and stuffed it back in his pocket.

"Where the hell is she?" he demanded furiously.

"I believe," Tallie said with a faint smile, "that on Fridays in the summer everyone has the afternoon off."

"Damn it!" Elias raked a hand through his hair, then stalked across the room to loom above her.

He wasn't actually *that* much taller than she was—four inches, maybe five—but he could loom with the best of them. She wondered if he'd taken looming lessons. Did they give looming lessons? Where?

Oh, God, she was losing her mind. She needed to get off her feet and get some drugs!

"I'll go get your pills. You sit down," Elias commanded.

"I'd love to," Tallie looked longingly at the armchair and sofa across the room.

Her apartment was bright and airy—and not a lot bigger than a postage stamp. Ordinarily. Now the sofa looked as far away as the moon. The armchair was in another galaxy. Harvey, after one curious glance in their direction, was in it, fast asleep.

Elias's gaze followed hers, then came back to zero in on her. "Give me the crutches."

"Why? So I can fall over?"

"No. I'll carry you. Give me the crutches."

"Don't be so bossy."

"Then fall over, damn it." He looked as if he'd rather strangle her than carry her. "I'll help you to the sofa, Prez, but not if you've got weapons."

"Oh." The penny dropped. And Tallie noticed suddenly that, even though he seemed to be looming, Elias was keeping out of her crutches' reach. "Once bitten, twice shy?" she ventured with a faint grin.

"Let's just say you're not getting another chance." There was a flicker of remembered pain in his eyes that made her momentarily remorseful. And she really did need to sit down.

"Here." She thrust them at him. He caught them and tossed them aside, then scooped her into his arms.

And for the second time she was in Elias Antonides's arms. Worse, she was glad to be there, grateful for the muscular hard strength of them cradling her, for the solid expanse of chest against which she leaned, for the strong firm jaw that—

*Whoa! Hold on a minute, girl!* The strong, firm jaw had nothing to do with him getting her to the sofa.

Of course, she knew that. She was just delirious with pain. Or…or something.

Still she was aware of feeling his heart beating as he carried her to the sofa. She watched his Adam's apple move when he swallowed as he lowered her onto the cushions. And she noticed that he had cut himself shaving. There was a tiny nick on the edge of his jaw. There was also a longer older scar on the underside of his chin.

Instinctively she touched it.

Elias jerked. His brows drew down.

"Sorry," Tallie said quickly. "I saw the scar. I just wondered… what happened?"

"When I was ten I stopped a hockey puck with my face."

"Ouch." The very thought made her wince.

"Yeah, that about covered it. No big deal," he said, echoing her earlier words.

He lowered her carefully to the sofa. His face was less than a foot from her own. And, scar and all, he was, without a doubt, the most handsome man she'd ever seen. Even her pain-fogged brain could register that. So did her body. All unbidden, it seemed to lean toward him.

Their eyes met. And something arced between them. Oh, help! But before she could bend her mind around it, Elias straightened quickly and stepped back. If she'd been a hot potato, he couldn't have backed off faster.

"I'll get you some pillows." He made a production of gathering up her assortment of gaily covered throw pillows from around the room and piled them at the foot of the sofa. When he had built a small mountain, he stepped back and waited for her to lift her ankle up onto it. It might as well have been Everest.

And Elias seemed to realize that at the same moment she did. Gently he grasped her ankle and carefully—hot potato carefully—lifted her casted ankle to rest on them.

"Thank you." Tallie breathed a sigh of relief.

"Okay. I'll go back to the office and get your pills. Don't go anywhere."

Tallie just looked at him. "As if."

He should send them back via messenger. Call a car and have the driver take them over and bring them up. It was smarter than going back himself.

It was bad enough to lust after Tallie Savas when she was across the room from him at a meeting—even though it was wholly inappropriate. But it was something else entirely, now that he knew just how soft and warm she really was.

The feel of her body against his chest as he had carried her to the taxi was imprinted on his memory. And the short journey from the door of the apartment to the sofa—which he'd been determined to do to prove to himself how unaffected by her charms he actually was—proved the complete opposite instead.

When he'd lowered her to the sofa, it was all he could do not to kiss her and lie right down beside her. Muscle memory, he assured himself. In the past whenever he'd lowered a woman to a sofa or bed, it had always been a prelude to joining her, to making love with her.

And there was a direction his thoughts definitely needed to stay away from. Make love with Tallie Savas? Ye gods.

Talk about complicating his life!

He'd get her pain pills—and her damned briefcase—and wish

her the joy of them. Then he'd go home and ring up what was her name—Denise? Patrice?

Oh, yeah. Clarice. The woman he'd met at the gym.

Right. He'd take Clarice out. And then go back to her place. And he wouldn't answer his phone this time! They would have an uninterrupted evening, and he would forget all about Tallie Savas's soft curves. It seemed like such a good idea he rang her from the office while he was picking up Tallie's pills.

"It's Elias," he said. "How about meeting me at Casey's? We could have a drink or two. Go out for dinner?"

"Sounds lovely," Clarice purred. "I will look forward to it."

So would he. And it didn't matter where it went after dinner, he told himself as he walked the six blocks back to Tallie's flat, as long as it blotted Tallie Savas's big brown eyes and kissable lips and soft breasts right out of his brain.

Tallie was still lying on the sofa with the cat—Harvey, she had called him—sprawled next to her. She had her ankle up on the pillow, but she was barefoot now—and she'd unpinned her hair. It cascaded in all its luxuriant tangled glory against the buttery tan leather as she held the phone to her ear.

All thoughts of Clarice went right out of Elias's head. Hell.

Tallie waggled her fingers at him, applauded the sight of the briefcase, then motioned frantically for the pill bottle and a glass of water. At the same time she continued talking on the phone.

"Yes, Mom," she was saying. "No, Mom."

Three bags full, Mom, her expression seemed to say.

Elias understood. Was it just Greek parents, he wondered, who were ready to step in at a moment's notice to run your life for you? He gave her a wry, knowing smile.

Tallie sighed and winced as she moved her leg. "I'm fine, Mom. Really. It's not a bad break. Of course I can manage. No, I don't need to come home. I *am* home!"

Elias went to the kitchen to get the glass of water. There was some baklava on a cake plate under glass. He remembered the baklava all too well. It was the one thing she'd brought in this week he'd been powerless to resist. Even now his stomach growled. Determinedly he ignored it and fetched the water, then opened Tallie's briefcase, took out the bottle of pills, shook one into his palm and carried them back to the living room.

Tallie was still on the phone. "No, Mom. You do not need to come and take care of me. I have help. Don't worry. There will be someone here."

She took the glass when Elias held it out, popped the pill and mouthed her thanks. "Look, Mom. I really have to go. I'll talk to you tomorrow. I love you, too, and Daddy. Be sure to tell Daddy everything is fine, too. Tell him *I'm* fine, and I'm taking care of business. Tell him he is *not* to meddle!" She hung up as if the receiver was on fire. "They think I'm seven," she grumbled.

"Parents do."

"I guess. It just gets old. Thank you for bringing my briefcase and my pills."

"Not a problem." Elias carried the glass back to the kitchen and put the bottle of pain medication on the counter. "You should do what she said, though," he counseled when he returned. "Rest. Take it easy. Don't overdo. It's a good thing you've got some help coming in. You'll need it."

"Yes, Daddy."

"Don't push your luck," Elias warned her. He didn't feel in the least fatherly, and he wished she'd stop stretching her arms over her head that way. It lifted her breasts, made them all too noticeable, made him remember their softness. "It's true," he insisted.

Tallie shifted on the sofa, tipped her head back against the cushions giving him a view of a long, elegant neck. She shut her eyes. "Mmm. Yeah."

What? No argument?

Then she opened them again and smiled at him. The painkillers must have kicked in. She sure hadn't smiled at him like that earlier. Earlier she'd tried to kill him. Or maim him at least. He winced now, remembering.

That had been bad. This—this staring at her, having her smile at him—was worse. This was temptation. God, her hair was gorgeous.

Elias wiped his palms down the sides of his khakis. "So," he said briskly, "is there anything I can get you before I take off."

"A pizza."

He stared. "A what?"

"A pizza." Tallie looked hopefully at him, then smiled. "I'm starving.  I ate half a grapefruit for breakfast. I thought I'd eat one of the cinnamon rolls at the office. But, well, we all know how that turned out." She grimaced. "And then you wouldn't let me have lunch with Martin."

Yeah, but still… "A pizza?"

"There's a pizza place right downstairs. If you don't mind?" she added hesitantly. It was the most hesitancy he'd heard from her since he'd met her. That little hint of vulnerability. Was she doing it on purpose?

Whatever she was doing, it was working.

Elias rubbed a hand against the back of his neck. "Oh, hell. All right."

He could bring her up a pizza and still get over to Casey's to meet Clarice when she got off work.

"Great! What do you like on your pizza?"

"What would *I*—?"

"You haven't had lunch, either," she reminded him, then squinted at him assessingly. "Are you the goat cheese and pineapple type?"

"I am the pepperoni type. With double cheese," he said flatly. "None of that sissy stuff."

Tallie laughed. "Whatever you want, then. Tell them to put it on my account."

The last thing he was going to do was let Tallie Savas pay for the pizza. He supposed he could eat a piece or two while he waited until whoever was coming to stay with her turned up.

"The number is on the refrigerator magnet." She waved a hand toward the kitchen. "Sal's All You Ever Wanted In A Pizza. You can call it in."

"I'll go down." If he was going to stay here, he needed a little space, a little breathing room. A little less Tallie. "Stay put."

She smiled and gave him a lady-of-the-manor wave of her hand. "I believe I will."

When he got back with the pizza half an hour later she was asleep. She looked younger and surprisingly defenseless but just as mindblowingly beautiful. He kept his distance. It was better that way. But then she opened her eyes and smiled vaguely at him. Her face was flushed. Her hair was everywhere.

"You," she told him, smiling muzzily when she saw the pizza box, "are a regular prince."

"And you're drunk on painkillers," Elias said. He could see it in her eyes, in the loopy smile she was giving him. He got plates from the kitchen and carried them and the pizza box over to the coffee table in front of the sofa and set them down. Then he opened the box.

Tallie leaned forward, sniffing appreciatively. "I looooove pepperoni. Martin thinks it's plebeian."

"Martin would. So... you and the Bore had pizza at the opera?"

"*De* Boer," Tallie corrected primly. Then after a moment, "Duh Bore." She giggled. It was a very girlish infectious giggle. Elias wasn't used to thinking of Tallie Savas as girlish any more than he was used to thinking of her as defenseless. He watched her warily.

"We had pizza for lunch one day. Martin likes Gorgon-Gorgonzola," Tallie stumbled over the word. Her eyes looked glassy. "And smoked oysters. He says they're an aphro—" she looked around the room for inspiration, found none and shrugged vaguely "—whatever."

"Aphrodisiac?" Elias didn't like the sound of that.

Tallie giggled again. "Silly, isn't it? Do you s'pose he needs aphro-whatevers?" Her voice was getting a little slurred.

If she didn't know, that was good.

"I wouldn't be surprised," Elias said.

Tallie nodded sagely. Big exaggerated nods, her chin bumping her chest. "Me, neither." She reflected on that while she chewed her pizza. "Do you need 'em?"

"*What?*" Elias dropped the pizza in his lap. "Damn it." He

jumped up, swiping ineffectually at the grease and tomato sauce with a paper towel.

Tallie watched his every move. Then she said, as if she'd been considering it, "No, you prob'ly don't." She looked straight at him. "You're pretty sexy as is."

Of course it was the painkiller talking, and she was going to regret like hell having said that in the morning—if she even remembered in the morning.

Elias rubbed a hand against the back of his neck. "Um, thanks. I think."

The loopy smile returned. "You're welcome." She looked at him expectantly.

He wished he knew what she was expecting. Then immediately he thought it was probably better that he didn't.

"Eat your pizza," he ordered gruffly.

Tallie smiled at him—one of those smiles that made all his hormones go on alert.

Deliberately he focused on his pizza. He finished it quickly, then wiped his hands on the paper towel and glanced at his watch. It was close to four and he had to go back to his place, grab a shower and change his clothes for something without tomato sauce before meeting Clarice.

Getting to his feet he said, "Look, I really should be heading out. When's your help coming?"

Tallie who had been dozing, opened her eyes and frowned. "My help?"

"You told your mother you were having help."

"I did. You. You brought pizza."

"Me? I'm not— Listen, Prez, you need someone with you."

"You're with me."

"I'm not staying."

"Oh." The light went out of her eyes.

Elias felt as if he'd taken candy from a child. He raked a hand through his hair. "I can't!"

"Of course." She waved a vague hand toward the door. "Well,

goodbye, then," And she dismissed him as if he didn't matter and went back to eating her pizza.

If anything proved that she shouldn't be left on her own, it was that. She didn't even know she needed to have someone there.

"Oh, hell." Elias stalked into the kitchen, grabbed his phone and punched in Clarice's number. When she answered, he said, "I can't make it. Something's come up. Business." This *was* business, damn it. Tallie was president of the company.

Clarice made a tsking sound. "Ah, *mon cher,* you work too hard. But," she reminded him, "at least this time it is not your mother."

No, God help him, it wasn't.

But this might well be worse.

# CHAPTER SIX

TALLIE was having the oddest dream.

She was dreaming she was swimming. But not swimming easily the way she always had. No, this time she was dragging an anchor, barely able to move. And though there was water, she was thirsty, parched, desperate for a drink.

She thrashed, trying to reach land, to reach the oasis, the cool shade of the beach and rest. And water. Dear God, she wanted water.

And then Elias Antonides, of all people, handed her a glass.

She took it, drank it quickly, took pills he offered her, let him wipe her forehead, let him straighten her pillows, let him shift the purple anchor and make the ache go away.

It was amazing how quickly it vanished.

Because Elias was there.

"Do you do magic?" she asked him.

"What?" He looked rumpled and worried. His shirt was hanging loose, and his tie was gone. There was a shadow of stubble on his jaw. He was even handsomer in her dreams than he was in real life. Figured.

He was nicer than he was in real life, too. She smiled muzzily at him. "You must do magic," she said. "You make the pain go away."

A corner of his mouth quirked. "Me and the little white pills."

She tried to focus on the pills. But she didn't see them clearly. It was because she was dreaming.

It was the first time she'd dreamed of Elias in her bedroom. Usually she had dreams about the two of them at work. Sometimes they were, um, interesting dreams. But they'd never gone as far as she'd have been interested in taking them. In her dreams, of course!

"Nice pills," she murmured.

"Apparently," Elias's tone was dry. But he was smiling at her. He almost never smiled at her. He had a lovely smile. "You might want to eat something with them," he suggested. "Are you hungry?"

"Don't want," she said, then frowned. What was it she remembered about pizza? Had she and Elias had pizza? No. She and Martin had had pizza. But she remembered something about Elias bringing her pizza.

Or maybe that was another dream. She tried to remember, but she was too tired. She shut her eyes. But she was hungry. His having mentioned food made her think about it.

"Baklava," she said woosily. She wondered if she had the strength to get up and get some. Maybe she could just dream she was eating it. That would be wonderful. But she didn't much feel like moving.

"Here." A gruff voice penetrated the fog that was her mind.

She opened her eyes. No, she didn't. She must be still dreaming because Elias was still here. In fact he was standing besides the bed with a plate of something in his hand.

She blinked at him. "Whazzat?"

"Baklava. You said you wanted some."

What a dream! What a spectacular dream. Not only was Elias Antonides starring in it, all rumpled and gorgeous looking, he was bringing her baklava in bed!

Tallie accepted the plate, but it wobbled precariously in her grasp.

"Here," he said. "Give it back." And the next thing she knew, he was holding the plate again and sitting beside her on the bed.

Bemused at how real it all seemed, albeit slightly fuzzy around the edges, Tallie took a piece of the baklava and bit into it. Ambrosial…if she did say so herself.

"Mmm." She shut her eyes, savoring the sweetness, and licked the honey off her lips. A slightly strangled sound made her open her eyes again. Elias was looking at her, a rather odd, definitely desperate look on his face.

"Oh," she said. "Sorry. I should have offered you some."

"No, it's okay. I'm—"

"You must be hungry. Eat." She held out what was left of her piece of baklava, waving it under his nose, brushing it against his lips.

"Tal—" But that was as far as he got, because she poked the baklava in his mouth. His lips touched her fingers. His mouth shut in surprise and he half coughed before he managed to swallow and then chew the unexpected treat. "Thank you," he said when he'd swallowed again. He sounded very polite and rather strained.

"Stop that," she told him.

His brow furrowed. "Stop what?"

"Acting all stiff and proper. This is my dream and you aren't supposed to behave that way."

He looked almost startled. But then he shrugged slightly and his lips quirked. "I'm not? How am I supposed to behave?"

"You're supposed to be nice," she told him firmly. "Well, you have been, I guess. Bringing me the baklava. But sometimes at work you're cranky."

"I apologize."

"See? There. You're doing it again. Smile," she commanded. He barred his teeth.

"Not like that. Are you ticklish?"

"What?" His eyes went wide.

"I asked if you were ticklish. If I tickled you and you laughed, that would be as good as a smile."

"I'm not ticklish," he said dampeningly.

"Pity." She picked up the last piece of baklava and broke it in two and held a piece of it out level with his mouth, inviting him to take another bite.

He hesitated a moment, then leaned forward and did just that.

Only this time he wasn't surprised. She was. Because this time he didn't just nibble at the baklava—he nibbled her fingers!

The feeling was so unexpected and so surprisingly intimate that she jerked back, shocked. "Elias!"

He grinned.

Oh my, yes. It was even better than a smile. Elias Antonides's grin was glorious. It was memorable. She hoped to goodness this was one of those dreams she could recall after she woke up!

"Here," he said, and began to brush the crumbs off the bed-clothes and into his hand. It necessitated him touching the light-weight duvet that was covering her. It necessitated him brushing his hands over her breasts, over her belly and her thighs. It seemed almost as intimate as his nibbling her fingers had.

And then, somehow he was leaning right over her, his face very close, nearly in her own, and his deep, dark eyes met hers, locked with hers. His lips were just inches from her own—right where they had been before he'd kissed her.

*Kissed her?*

What?

Good Lord, another dream? A dream within a dream? She blinked rapidly. Gave her head a little shake.

Elias straightened up. "What's wrong? Got something in your eye?"

Tallie shook her head again, dazed, trying to think. To remember. But it was gone. Whatever she'd thought she was remembering she couldn't.

It was just the feeling, she thought. It was how she used to feel when Brian had kissed her. There had been that moment of connection, of anticipation, of need. That was what she was remembering!

She was missing Brian. Her gaze sought the picture on her dresser. It was too dark in the room, though, with only the small reading lamp illuminated. She couldn't see her 5-by-7 inch Brian in the shadows. She could only see Elias, tall and strong and dev-astatingly sexy, looking down at her worriedly.

He was too vivid, too present to allow her to focus on any-thing—or anyone—else. Memories of Brian slid away as memories of Brian had been doing lately. And this was only a dream, anyway.

She might as well enjoy her dream.

She reached out and took hold of his shirtfront and pulled him down toward her again.

"Tallie?"

"Shh. Just testing," she murmured, and then she pressed her lips to his.

It was indeed the dream to end all dreams, she thought dizzily as the kiss went on and on and became better and better.

Even dreaming she remembered thinking he was the last man in the world she ought to have anything to do with. But Elias Antonides kissed as good as he looked. Better, in fact. The best since Brian.

Possibly, her traitorous thoughts proclaimed, even better than Brian—though she *loved* Brian.

Still, she had to admit, for a dream kiss, it was the best she'd ever had. She didn't know why she didn't dream about kissing more often if she was so good at conjuring up kisses like this!

The last man she'd kissed for real had been Martin—if you could call the dry press of his mouth against hers a kiss. What she remembered most about that was the aftertaste of goat cheese.

Elias's kiss, on the other hand, was the sort she could take out and replay to keep her warm on subzero nights in Antarctica. Con Ed could use it to light up all of Manhattan and have enough wattage left over for Brooklyn and the Bronx besides.

It threatened to burn them both right down to the ground. And Tallie knew she would go willingly and die with a smile on her face.

Her hands slid underneath his shirt. She ran her fingers through the soft, springy hair on his chest, savored the heat of his body, the ripple of his muscles as he caught his breath. His fingers came up to tangle in her hair, to weave and thread and curl the strands, to tug lightly on them, to bring her closer, to bring the two of them together.

She wanted more. She wanted it all. And so, it seemed, did

he. But as she began to fumble with his buttons, there was a thump, and Harvey—her subscious in feline form, no doubt—landed on the bed. A shred of sanity reminding her that even in her dreams there were some things she shouldn't do.

Apparently, the dream Elias thought the same thing because he pulled back abruptly, then stared at her looking as dazed as she was. She was aware—and pleased—that he looked as shattered as she felt. At least in her dreams she could disconcert him.

"Bad idea, Prez. Really, really bad," he said raggedly. And then he'd straightened up and walked out of the room.

Watching him go, Tallie found herself wishing that her subconscious cat hadn't disturbed them. It would have been more than interesting to make love with Elias Antonides. She touched her tingling lips, thinking how real they felt, how well kissed.

"Killjoy," she muttered to Harvey.

Then she closed her eyes and willed herself back into the dream, curious now. If she could get back to the level where she and Elias were kissing, well, she thought with a smile, she might never want to wake up.

Unfortunately she did.

Her ankle was throbbing. It took her a moment to figure out why. To remember the accident. The ambulance. The hospital. The purple Barney of a cast that felt like a lead weight on her leg. The meeting at the office. That mortifying journey out of the building and the trip home in the taxi with Elias and then him having to go back and get her pain pills for her.

Thank God today was Saturday. She wouldn't have to face him again until Monday.

Wincing, Tallie carefully rolled her aching bruised body over in her bed and stared in horror at the rumpled, stubble-jawed man sound asleep in *Yiayia* Savas's old rocking chair next to her bed.

Oh, dear God.

Tallie squeezed her eyes shut, disbelieving the sight before her eyes, trying desperately to subdue the pounding behind her eyelids that seemed to make her hallucinate. But when she opened them again, he was still there—Elias Antonides!—in her bedroom!

But…that was a dream!

Please, God, it had been a dream!

But even as she thought it, Tallie had a gut-twisting feeling that it hadn't been a dream at all. Her heart hammered. That was anxiety. Her head pounded. She felt as if she had the mother of all hangovers. And that was, she knew, the aftereffects of the pain medication.

She never should have taken any. The pills worked—good heavens, yes, she knew they worked. Give her one and she was blessedly pain free—but they also did a number on her head.

She knew from past experience that they made her hazy, blurry, loopy, crazy and absolutely irresponsible for anything that she said or did.

Which was exactly why she'd refused to take any until she got home. She had known she would need all her wits about her at the office. She would never have been able to pay attention or make sense if her brain was buzzing. That was why she'd rung her parents, too, before Elias had returned with them. She wanted to sound with it and sensible so they wouldn't come and hover over her.

So she'd got, what? Elias instead?

Dear God.

A kaleidoscope of more dizzy impressions crowded into her still-pounding head. She tried to think, to sort, to remember. He'd brought her the pills she'd left in her briefcase at the office. He'd brought her pizza. A good satisfying pepperoni pizza with lots of gooey cheese, not one of those designer pizzas like she and Martin the Bore—*de Boer*—had shared, and she'd told him about Martin and the aphrodisiacs and—

Her face burned as she remembered that conversation.

And then, blessedly, Elias had said he had to leave. But he'd been determined to wait for the person coming to take care of her. And she'd had to admit she'd made it up to reassure her mother.

"You mean no one will be here?" he'd demanded.

And when she'd shaken her head, assuring him she'd be fine, he'd snorted and stalked off to the kitchen. She vaguely remembered him cleaning up the pizza and talking on the phone. And then he'd come back and sat down in the chair opposite the sofa.

"Go away," she'd said.

But of course he hadn't listened. He'd picked up a magazine and had started to read. She didn't remember anything more because the bloody little pill had done its trick and she'd fallen asleep on the sofa.

But she wasn't on the sofa now. She was in her bed—in a nightgown she couldn't remember putting on—and a man she remembered dreaming about kissing was no dream at all. He was sound asleep barely a foot away.

Tallie moaned.

Elias jerked. His eyes flicked open. For just an instant he looked as confused as she'd been feeling, but then clarity unclouded his gaze and he pushed himself upright. "You're awake. You need another pill?" He was already heading on autopilot for wherever he'd put them.

"No!" Good God, no! She'd made a big enough idiot of herself already.

At her desperate shout he turned back. "You sure?" He sounded doubtful.

His dark hair was sticking up in spikes. His shirttails hung out. Only three buttons were done up on his shirt and his tie was gone. The stubble on his jaw was even darker than it had been when she'd kissed him—

Remembering that it wasn't a dream, Tallie moaned again.

"I'm getting you a pill," Elias said.

"No! Really. I don't need any pills. I'm…fine." She struggled to push herself up against the headboard of her bed.

Elias moved to help her, then stopped abruptly, jammed his hands in the pockets of his khakis and remained where he was.

Probably afraid he was going to get attacked again. Should she acknowledge what she'd done? Pass it off with a laugh? Or was it better to pretend it had never happened?

Because one look at him told her that, no matter how gorgeous he was and how tempting it would be to kiss him again, Elias had no desire for a repeat performance.

Nor did she! He was the man her father had set his sights on for her. She didn't love him. She was attracted to him—on a purely physical level. And that was all. She loved Brian.

Who was dead, a tiny voice inside her head reminded her.

True. But even so…she did *not* love Elias Antonides! Getting involved with him would be disastrous. It would complicate everything.

*And* it would make her father even more power-mad than he already was.

So, what was she going to do about the kiss?

Nothing. Elias had to know she hadn't meant it, that if she'd been in her right mind, she'd never have done it. So if she acted as if she didn't remember, they would both be spared some needless embarrassment. And if he should happen to bring it up, she could laugh it off, say she'd been "under the influence."

It was nothing but the truth.

"So," Elias said, "fine. No pills. Can I get you some water?"

"That would be nice." She gave him a polite determinedly distant smile. "Thank you."

He nodded wordlessly and left the room. When he came back with a glass of water, he had his shirt buttoned and neatly tucked in. He'd run his fingers through his hair, and while he hadn't necessarily tamed it, he looked proper and quite as determined to get things back on a businesslike footing as she was.

As it should be, Tallie reminded herself.

She drank the whole glass of water, handed it back, then looked up at him with what she hoped was the proper degree of businesslike equanimity. "It was very kind of you to stay last night."

"Not a problem."

"Still," she insisted, "you didn't have to."

Elias shrugged. "Somebody did."

Tallie was tempted to dispute that. But Elias didn't look as though he was going to give in on that argument. And if she tried, things might be brought up she had no desire to discuss. So she merely inclined her head. "Yes, well, it was above and beyond the call of duty. Thank you."

His mouth twisted briefly and she wondered which "beyond the call of duty" moments he was remembering. But he simply nodded. "You're welcome."

Their gazes met, locked. And the notion that painkillers had been solely responsible was hard to accept.

Abruptly Elias looked away. "So, you're okay today?" he asked briskly, all business. "How's your ankle?"

"It hurts, but I can live with it. No problem." Every muscle in her body ached, in truth. "I'll be fine."

"Right. Well then, I guess I'll take off. He sat down in the rocking chair and yanked on his socks and shoes, then stood up again. "If you decide you need them, your pills are by the sink in the bathroom. Your crutches are here by the bed." He poked them with his toe. "And your cell phone is on the nightstand. Do you want me to get you something to eat before I leave?"

"No, I can get something later."

"Sure?"

"Absolutely. Again, thank you very much."

It was all very polite now. Very businesslike and distant. And awkward as hell because she could remember the sandpapery feel of his jaw against her cheek, could remember the hungry press of his lips. And wanted, heaven help her, to feel them again.

She cleared her throat. "I'll see you Monday."

Elias opened his mouth, started to speak, then closed it again and nodded. "Right. See you Monday. Take care."

The woman was going to be the death of him—or at least of his better intentions!

Elias needed the whole weekend to recover his equilibrium, to stop remembering the taste of Tallie Savas's lips, the softness of her body, the smoothness of her skin.

Well, he did remember. But for odd isolated moments now and then he managed to focus on something else.

It took some effort.

Saturday, as soon as he left Tallie's apartment, he started working on the offices he was renovating. But that gave him far too much time on his own. Way too much opportunity to remember the way he'd spent the night—and how much more he'd wanted to do with Tallie that night.

And even reminding himself that he hadn't wanted to do it because it was *Tallie* and it would have been a huge mistake didn't give him reason enough to forget how much he'd enjoyed her touch, her kiss—*her!*

So he rang Dyson and woke him up. "You still want to show me that boat you're having built?"

A trip out to Long Island to see Dyson's pride and joy had been on the back burner too long. Dyson had invited him to come along to see it half a dozen times. But every time Elias had been too busy.

Now he heard Dyson yawn so loudly his jaw cracked. Then Dyson said, "Yeah. Pick you up in an hour."

They spent the day at the boatyard, which made Elias remember how much he had loved building boats with his grandfather and how sidetracked his life had become. Thinking about the past gave him some respite from memories of Tallie in his arms.

But it also reminded him of other dreams he'd had—of a life split between Santorini and New York, of building boats for a living, of marrying a woman who would love the same things he did and the family they would have together.

It hadn't happened the way he'd imagined. Not any of it.

And the memories of what he'd hoped for and what had actually happened made him surly.

"Not gonna bring you again," Dyson said on the way home. "You been scowling all day long. You look like hell, too. What'd you do last night?"

"Nothing," Elias said, staring out the window at the traffic heading into the city. It was the truth. He hadn't done what he'd wanted to do for a long, long time.

It was his own fault, of course. No one had forced him to do any of it. No one had held a gun to his head and made him marry Millicent. No one had demanded he take over Antonides Marine and abandon his dreams of his own boat-building business.

And no one would have stopped him if he'd made love with Tallie Savas last night—least of all Tallie.

It was his own bloody misguided sense of doing what was right. He needed to get over it, get past it, get a life. If he had a woman, he wouldn't be tempted by the likes of Tallie Savas.

So as soon as Dyson dropped him off, he rang Clarice.

"How about tonight?" he asked her. "I'll leave my phone at home. No mothers. No sisters. No business."

And definitely no Tallie!

*"Mais, oui,"* Clarice said in her honeyed voice. "I would like that."

So would he, Elias promised himself. So would he.

He picked her up just before eight. They had a good meal. Very elegant. Very French. They had some interesting conversation. At least he thought they did. The trouble was, he kept losing his train of thought. His brain kept flashing back to the night before—to the pizza he'd shared with Tallie, to the totally nonsensical conversation they'd had when she hadn't been falling asleep—

"But you see, it is still a problem," Clarice said sadly.

Elias's mind jerked back to the present. "Problem?" What had he missed? "What problem?"

"The business," Clarice explained. "You said there would be no business. And yes, there is no business here. But you think about it—" she tapped the side of her head "—here, anyway."

He could hardly say it wasn't *business* he was thinking about!

His mouth twisted wryly. "I'm sorry. I'm just…distracted. We could go somewhere," he suggested, reaching for her hand across the table. "Do something that would blot business right out of my mind."

He was sure she knew what he meant. But she smiled ruefully and shook her head. "I would invite you back to my place," Clarice said, "but my sister is visiting from Paris."

"So you can come to mine."

Another shake of her head. "Not when my sister is visiting," Clarice said. "I cannot be gone all night."

Elias squeezed her hand. "Another time?"

She gave him a brilliant smile. "But of course."

He took her home and did manage at least to get a kiss before he left her on her doorstep. He told himself it was a start. But it might have been one more mistake, because it made him think about Tallie's kiss. This one was nowhere near as memorable.

No matter, he told himself resolutely as he walked home. He had a woman in his life again—a woman who promised a casual, easy relationship with no demands, no strings, no expectations.

Exactly what he wanted.

Monday brought Tallie in bright and early, as usual. With a Viennese delicacy, as usual. With carrot and celery sticks for him—as usual. She was bouncy and perky and, other than the silly purple cast on her ankle, she looked cheerful and well rested—as if Friday night had never happened at all.

Good. Because he wasn't going to think about it. Or her. He'd had two days to put the matter in perspective. And he had decided on the best course—he would forget it. And other than professionally, where he had no choice, he would ignore her.

Which was easier said than done when she was sitting right across from him at a two-hour meeting and his mind kept flashing back to memories of what it had felt like to tangle his fingers in her wild, untamable hair.

It was pinned and anchored today, of course. Only a few tendrils were escaping, but Elias's fingers clenched into fists as he remembered the silken softness of those tendrils, the vibrant springiness of them, the total temptation of them—

He jerked his thoughts back to the subject at hand. He didn't look at Tallie again. He was tempted. He resisted.

He was almost grateful when Rosie appeared halfway through the meeting to get him to take an urgent call. He was less grateful when it turned out to be Cristina.

"I need to talk to you!"

"Now?"

"You haven't been answering your phone. I've been calling you for days."

"I'm busy." And he'd had no desire to spend his weekend mopping up a series of family disasters. Besides the flood of messages from Cristina, there had been several from Lukas about problems in New Zealand, a half a dozen from Martha demanding that he call her, a surprising message from his brother Peter suggesting that they talk, and, of course, the requisite dinner invitation from his mother who wanted him to meet someone called Augusta, whom she described as his "soul mate." Elias seriously doubted that. Why would he want to answer any of them?

"Too busy for your family?" Cristina demanded.

Yes, damn it. "I'm in a meeting. What do you want?"

There was an infinitesimal pause. Then, "I want you to hire Mark."

"And I want a roast duck to fly over and fall into my mouth. Come on, Cristina. Get real. Not going to happen."

"See," she wailed. "I knew you'd do that. You won't even consider it!"

"No."

"But—"

"No, Cristina. I have to go. People are waiting." He drummed his fingers on Rosie's desk and glared at her for calling him out of the meeting.

"She said it was urgent," Rosie mouthed at him.

"You don't know him!" Cristina waited.

"I do know him," Elias reminded her. "That's the problem."

"But I love him!"

She *loved* Mark Batakis? Ye gods. Elias grimaced, then pinched the bridge of his nose and drew a deep breath. "And your undying love gives him what sort of job qualifications?" he asked politely.

"I don't know!" Cristina's voice wobbled. "But you don't have to be a smart-ass. Mark is no dummy. He can learn anything. He went to Yale after all. And…and he knows a lot about boats."

"He *races* boats, Cristina. Not the same thing."

"But boats are—"

"Cristina," Elias said with all the patience he could muster, "we *don't* race boats. We have nothing to do with racing boats."

"We could," she insisted.

"We could build a rocket ship and fly to the moon, too. But we're not going to."

"Even so. All I'm asking is for you to talk to him," Cristina said tightly.

"And give him a job."

"Well, yes, but—"

"No. Besides," he said with considerable relish, "even if I wanted to, I can't."

"You mean you won't!"

"No, I mean I can't." For the first time Elias felt kindly toward his father's idiotic bet with Socrates Savas. "I'm not the boss anymore."

"What do you mean you're not the boss?" Cristina demanded.

"Didn't you hear? Dad sold forty percent of the business."

"What? Dad *sold*—" His sister sputtered her disbelief.

"Sold," Elias reiterated. "Which makes him no longer president."

"Then you're—"

"No, I'm not," he said with considerable satisfaction. "You want to get your boyfriend a job at Antonides Marine, Cristina, you'll have to talk to the new CEO."

There was a pause, then Cristina said stoutly, "All right. I will. What's his name?"

"*Her* name is Tallie Savas."

It was going to be all right.

Tallie kept telling herself that as she kept trying to convince herself—and Elias—that she had no memory of what had happened that night in her apartment. She had come in today determined to act as if nothing at all had occurred.

And she thought Elias believed it.

He looked at her oddly once or twice, but when she gave no sign, he focused on business.

She wished she could.

She wished she could stop remembering how he had kissed her, how firm and warm his lips had been, how springy his hair was, how rough his stubbled jaw had been, how hot his skin had felt beneath her fingers.

She wished—

She wished a lot of things—mostly that she'd never heard of Antonides Marine, that she had never taken this job, that she had never met Elias Antonides. He made her want the things she had wanted with Brian, things she'd put aside after Brian's death, things she had promised herself she would only want again if another man worthy to step into Brian's shoes came into her life—a man who loved her for herself, who wanted her and not her father's money or his empire.

A man, in short, who was nothing like Elias Antonides!

She knew he didn't want her father's money or his empire. He simply wanted his own empire back! But he didn't want her—not in the way Brian had. He didn't care about her. Only about sex.

She wondered why he'd stopped.

God knew she wouldn't have been able to. She'd been daft enough to think Harvey was her subconscious alter ego, her common sense. Under the influence of painkillers she didn't have the common sense of a cat!

A thought that didn't make her feel any better.

At least spending time watching how her father handled himself in business had taught her that it was wise to give nothing away, to maintain her cool, to appear indifferent and unconcerned at all costs.

So she'd done that. She'd come bearing *apfelstrudel,* had chatted easily with Rosie and Lucy, had endured Dyson's teasing about losing a battle with a truck and had deflected Paul's sympathy for her pain by joking about her "Barney cast."

And she'd smiled politely at Elias. He had smiled politely at her. Sanity prevailed.

All the same she was glad when he had to go out of their meeting briefly to take a phone call. It was easier to concentrate when he wasn't in the room. When he came back, she felt immediately edgy and aware again. She forced herself to concentrate on Paul's charts and diagrams and endless monotonous commentary. She even managed to make a couple of points herself about her concern that Corbett's, while a good business in itself, was perhaps not the direction Antonides wanted to go in.

"Why not?" Elias demanded.

And so she explained her feeling of enervation. "And it's not just me," she said. "No one here is particularly excited about this. No one is champing at the bit to buy in."

"We're taking our time," Elias said, "working out the ramifications. Crunching the numbers."

"Fine," Tallie said. "But you've got to have more than numbers, even if they add up. You've got to want to do this, you've got to want to make seaworthy apparel."

Elias just stared at her as if she was crazy.

"You do," Tallie insisted. "You need passion." And then she remembered another kind of passion they had shared the other night and her face flamed. She could actually *feel* the heat of the blood that rushed to her face. She pressed her lips together and focused on Paul, on Dyson, on anyone or anything but Elias. "I think Corbett's is fine as a business, but maybe not *our* business," she added quickly. "I just don't think any of us wants to commit."

When she finally dared venture a glance in Elias's direction, he was staring at the whiteboard behind Paul, as if he were deliberately not remembering Friday night, too. Thank God.

Finally he looked around the room. No one else said anything either. "Yes? No?" They all looked at each other.

Dyson cleared his throat. "She might be right," he said slowly. "I mean, we've gone back to the drawing board on it how many times?"

"Lots," Paul muttered.

Elias didn't look totally convinced, but he didn't disagree, either. "Okay. I told Corbett we'd let him know," he said, finally allowing his gaze to meet Tallie's. "We can talk about it in the morning." He shoved back his chair and stood up. "Right now Dyson and I are heading out to Long Island."

Tallie felt an enormous sense of relief. So he wasn't going to be in the office all afternoon? Yippee. "What's there?"

"Nikos Costanides's boatyard."

"*The* Nikos Costanides?"

Elias raised his brows. "You know him?"

"Of him." Right around the time she had met Brian, Nikos had been on her father's short list of eligible Greeks. Because of Brian she'd never met him. Just as well because she had never been in Nikos Costanides's league. While she had been dating her Navy pilot, Nikos had been squiring around some of the world's most gorgeous women and being written up in scandal sheets on both sides of the Atlantic.

After Brian's death, when her father was again compiling his list, she learned that Nikos, the wild playboy, had in the meantime married, settled down, had kids and, thus, permanently removed himself from her father's eligible list.

"We went out and looked at the boat he's building for Dyson on the weekend." There was a light in his eyes that Tallie hadn't seen before. "You might be right about the enthusiasm bit," he told her.

"Oh?"

"We'll see. I'll leave my notes for you and we can go over them tomorrow morning, then call Corbett."

Tallie nodded. "That will be fine." Very proper. Very cool. Very businesslike. Whew.

Elias opened the door and she preceded him into the main reception area. A young woman was sitting there, idly flipping through a magazine.

"Nine o'clock? I'll just—" Elias broke off as the woman stood up. He scowled furiously at her. "What the hell are you doing here?"

"Nice to see you again, too, Elias, dear." She gave him a brilliant smile, sashayed toward him and kissed him on the cheek.

She was one of the most gorgeous women Tallie had ever seen. Tall and striking, with short spiky dark hair that had the casual ruffled elegance that only came with a high price tag, and cheekbones you only saw in magazine ads. Everything about her, from her trendy clothes to her perfectly applied makeup added up to make her one stunning young woman—exactly the sort who would attract a man like Elias. Even though he didn't seem especially delighted to see her, there was no denying they made a spectacular couple.

Was she the woman he'd stood up on Friday night?

Tallie vaguely remembered him making a phone call, telling someone he couldn't make something, apologizing. Maybe she'd told him off and they'd had a fight and that was why he was glowering at her now.

"Go home," he said brusquely.

"No. I won't. You said talk to the president!"

Elias's expression darkened. "For God's sake—"

"President?" Tallie frowned.

The young woman's gaze fixed on her, brown eyes alight with curiosity. "Is this—"

"Yes," Elias said through his teeth. "It is. And you can't talk to her now. She's busy."

"She doesn't look busy," the young woman said matter-of-factly. "Are you?" she asked Tallie.

"It's lunchtime," Elias said.

"Then we'll have lunch." She held out her hand to Tallie. Her nails were well shaped and beautifully manicured. Tallie's were short and utilitarian, good for kneading pastry dough. "I'm Cristina."

"Cristina?" Tallie looked to Elias for an explanation.

She got one—short and furious. "My sister!"

# CHAPTER SEVEN

TALLIE Savas was having lunch with his sister.

The very thought made the hair on the back of Elias's neck stand straight up. What Cristina, with her big mouth and her ungovernable brain, might do or say to Tallie was horrifying to contemplate. There were plenty of loose-cannon genes in the Antonides family, but Cristina's were the loosest.

He had half a mind not to go to Long Island with Dyson at all. But he could hardly change his mind when Tallie was smiling delightedly and saying she'd *love* to have lunch with Cristina, and his sister was grinning like the Cheshire Cat and waggling her fingers at him and saying not to worry at all, that she knew just the place to take the new president of Antonides Marine.

He shuddered to think. In fact, he expected to spend the entire day distracted by what was happening back in Brooklyn.

But Nikos Costanides was a compelling man.

Elias had never met him before Saturday when Nikos had dropped by the boatyard to pick something up and had found Dyson there showing Elias his new, nearly finished boat. A twenty-two-foot gaff-rigged sailboat, it was every bit as fantastic as Dyson had claimed it would be. And when Nikos, who had only come to pick up some files he'd left at the office, discovered that Elias had a serious boat-building background, he'd invited them back this afternoon. And he was waiting for them when they arrived, eager to show them around.

Costanides Custom Boats was the stuff of Elias's childhood dreams. That it should have apparently been Nikos's dream, too, surprised him. While he hadn't known Nikos, he was acquainted with Stavros Costanides, Nikos's father. The elder Costanides was a friend of his own father. They played golf together now and then. It was always interesting to watch them because Aeolus always tried hard and enjoyed the exercise, and Stavros Costanides was there to win. No more, no less. He was everything Elias's father was not—tough, astute, hard as nails.

Nikos, from everything Elias had been, was a far different story. He was the star of every cautionary tale Elias had ever been told. Stories of Nikos the wild care-for-nothing playboy, bane of his father's existence, were legion and oft repeated.

"You don't be like that Nikos Costanides," his mother had said, shaking her finger at him. "You settle down with a nice girl. You work hard. You take care of business."

God knew he'd tried. He'd done everything the family had ever expected him to—and more. He'd had no choice, of course. Not if Antonides Marine were going to survive. For all the good it had done him.

Nikos, he decided, had got the better deal.

All those years he'd spent avoiding working for his old man—"the only work that matters" according to Stavros Costanides—Nikos had not simply spent squiring beautiful women around. He had been working as hard as his old man, just not for Costanides International. Virtually tossed out on his ear because he wouldn't toe the familial line, Nikos had gone to university in Glasgow to train as a naval architect, then set up a custom boat-building business with a friend in Cornwall.

He'd made a success of his business and of his life—on his own terms.

Elias wished he could have done the same. He'd longed to make his mark the way Nikos had—to build boats the way Nikos had—and then come into the family business when he was ready.

If he were given to envy, Elias could have envied Nikos

Costanides. For his fiscally healthy, financially sound Costanides empire. For his thriving custom-boat business. For his whole life.

Because Nikos had one.

His smiling dark-haired wife, Mari, and his three little stair-step sons came by the boatyard that afternoon on their way home from the dentist.

"I promised them if they were brave we'd come see Daddy," Mari told Elias and Dyson, watching with undisguised adoration as the three little boys clambered all over Nikos who clearly doted on them.

It was the life Elias had once envisioned he would have with Millicent. But when he'd had to drop out of school to take over at Antonides Marine, things had changed. Even then, he'd have been happy to have a child.

"Why not?" he'd said to Millicent. "It will give me someone to work for. It won't be just for the past. It will be for the future."

But Millicent had been horrified. "Bring a child into this chaos? Absolutely not!"

"Chaos?" Elias hadn't seen it that way. He'd seen it as a challenge, a whole hell of a lot of work, to be sure, but also as an opportunity, a way to do something important for his family.

"Everything's about your family," Millicent had complained.

Yes, it was. But she was a part of his family. It wasn't just about his parents and siblings. It was about making a future for her and their children, as well.

But Millicent didn't want anything to do with that. She hadn't, in very short order, wanted anything to do with him.

Antonides Marine, in its faltering state, wasn't the shining company she'd thought it was. So Elias wasn't the man she'd hoped he would be. No matter that he was doing his damnedest to bring it back, to make it work.

She didn't want it. She didn't want him.

She wanted a divorce.

He hadn't believed it when she'd told him. He'd argued passionately that it wasn't too late to work things out. "We can get counseling. We can make it work," he'd told her.

But she'd said no. Just no. She'd left him. Gone to California where her parents lived. And when he'd finally found her again, she'd still refused to come back to him.

"It's too late," she said. She didn't love him anymore. There was someone else.

And she was going to have his child.

*His* child. She'd been willing to bring a child into that, but not into her marriage to Elias!

The memory still had the power to cut him to the core.

So he didn't think about it. He'd moved on. And for the most part he forgot about it. But sometimes it came back to haunt him—like today when he'd seen Nikos and Mari and their boys.

And last Friday night in Tallie Savas's bedroom.

He shoved the thought away.

They got back into the city shortly before eight. Dyson dropped him off and went to pick up a date and tell her all about his beautiful boat.

Elias went back to the office and did what he did every night. He went to work.

The place was totally quiet. Everyone else had long since gone home. There were half a dozen messages on his desk and another dozen on his answering machine. He ran through them quickly, relieved that none was from Tallie complaining about his idiot sister.

None was from Cristina, either, also a good thing. It meant that Tallie had taken her duties as president seriously and had sent Cristina and her boat-racing, job-seeking boyfriend packing with enough firmness that Cristina now knew that calling him wasn't going to get her anywhere.

Hallelujah.

Instinctively he reached for the phone to call Tallie and thank her, then changed his mind. He wasn't contacting Tallie outside of business hours. But since he had the phone in his hand, he rang one of the sail suppliers in San Diego instead.

All the workaholics on the West Coast were still in their offices. He spent two hours on the phone with one after another. He got a lot of work done.

What else did he have to do with his life?

It was almost ten when he finally quit. The muscles in his neck were knotted. His back ached. He flicked off the light in his office and headed for the door. On his way out, he spied a single piece of Tallie's apple strudel sitting on the plate by the break room.

He hadn't eaten any this morning. It had been a matter of self-control. He wasn't going to be seduced by Tallie Savas in any way, shape or form.

Tonight he was hungry. He hadn't had any dinner. Mari Costanides had invited them to the house for a meal, but they'd declined.

Now he stared at the pastry and his stomach growled, tempted. He glared at it. It wasn't the apple in the Garden of Eden, for heaven's sake! Just a simple piece of pastry. He was making way too much of it.

Screw it, he thought, grabbed the strudel and took a savage bite, then stomped up the stairs.

When he'd bought the old warehouse, it had seemed like a terrific idea—renovate it, use part of it for the Antonides Marine offices, rent out enough of the rest to other businesses to pay the mortgage, and keep a loft apartment for himself upstairs. Very neat, very efficient.

He couldn't get away from work even if he tried.

He unlocked the door to his apartment and pushed it open.

When Elias had started renovations, he'd had great plans for his own space. Working with wood had always reminded him of boyhood days spent working with his grandfather on Santorini. It was as close to doing what he'd always wanted to do as he was ever going to get. So the first thing he'd done, once the walls were up, plastered and painted, was to order the wood and build a bar of quarter-sawn oak between the living room and kitchen. Then he'd built matching oak cabinets and installed them, as well.

The rest of the furnishings—the sofa, armchair, two bar stools and a bed—were utilitarian. But he'd begun to put up a wall of bookshelves when business had demanded more attention again a few months ago.

Five months later a lot of his belongings were still in boxes stacked in the shadows against the walls. Other than the mural of Santorini and the sea that he'd hired his sister Martha to paint on one wall, nothing else had been done.

It wasn't a home. It was a camping spot.

And he wasn't in it alone.

Someone was sitting in the shadows on the sofa. It was a woman—slowly starting to get up.

"Martha?"

"No, it's Tallie." She settled her crutches under her arms and crossed the room into the light.

Elias stared in disbelief. *"Tallie?"*

She put a finger to her lips and almost lost a crutch. "Shh. Not so loud. You'll wake her."

"What?" He stared. "Wake who?"

"Cristina." She tipped her head in the direction of his bedroom. "Your sister."

As if there were another one.

"What the hell is Cristina doing here? Why's she in my bedroom?"

"Shh!" Tallie hissed. "I told you—" she grabbed his arm hard enough to make him wince "—you have to be quiet. You'll wake her up."

"You're damned right I'll wake her up! What's she doing in my apartment? In my bed?"

Tallie didn't answer. She began pulling him into the kitchen—or trying to. She wasn't having much luck with doing anything but banging his shins with her crutches as she made the attempt.

"For God's sake, stop that! All right." He turned her and got her balanced on her crutches again, standing right in front of him. "I'm not shouting. What's going on? Is she sick?"

"No, she's not sick."

"Then what—?"

Tallie looked at him nervously. "It's…complicated. Well—" she balanced on one crutch and shoved a hand through her cloud of dark hair "—maybe it's not that complicated, but…would you like a cup of tea or something?"

"Tea?" He gaped. "What you talking about?"

"Tea is good in crises."

That this was a crisis seemed to go without saying. "I don't have tea."

"You do now," Tallie informed him, nodding at the box on the counter. She turned her back to hobble to the stove and put on a kettle he'd never seen before, either. There were two mugs there, as well. Those he recognized. Obviously already used. As he watched, she opened the door to one of his cupboards and got out another mug.

"Made yourself at home, did you?"

"I didn't think you'd mind," she said, then turned and gave him an arch look, "since you did the same at my place."

Elias scowled, then stuffed his hands in his pockets and rocked back on his heels. "Okay, fine. We'll have a cup of tea. And then you can tell me what the hell is going on and what my bloody sister is doing here."

"Well, that part's easy. She's waiting for Mark."

"Mark?" Elias practically shouted. "What's he coming for?"

Tallie made shushing gestures again. "He's coming to get her. But he's out in Greenport. Or he was. I didn't reach him until seven."

Why she'd bothered to reach him at all was a mystery to Elias. One of many, apparently. He waited until the water boiled and then he picked up the kettle before she could, so she didn't scald herself by trying to stand up on crutches and pour boiling water at the same time.

"Thank you," she said. "It's a little awkward."

"As I'm sure you know. You poured for Cristina, didn't you?"

Tallie looked away. "She was upset. She wasn't feeling well—"

"I thought you said she wasn't sick?"

"Upset and sick are not the same thing. Don't worry. She's going to be fine."

"Terrific," he said sarcastically. Elias picked up the two mugs and jerked his head toward the sofa in the living room. "Come on."

He set the steaming mugs on the packing box he was currently using for a coffee table, then waited until Tallie sat down clumsily on the sofa. For a brief moment he debated picking up his own mug again and going to sit far away from her in the chair. It would be the sane, sensible thing to do.

But sane and sensible had pretty much gone out the door when he'd come in and found Tallie in his apartment. So he deliberately sat down on the sofa and turned toward her. "All right. Let's hear it."

Tallie took a deep breath. "Well, as you know, we went out for lunch. To this place in the East Village Cristina knew. Very funky. New. Trendy. Like her."

"Uh-huh."

"And we got to know each other a bit. I like Cristina. She's very funny, your sister."

"A laugh a minute," Elias said drily.

Tallie shot him a disapproving look. "She thinks you don't like her."

"I love her. She just drives me crazy. She doesn't have a practical bone in her body. She flits from one thing to the next. And she always expects me to fund whatever stupid scheme she's got lined up next."

"Yes, that's what she said." Tallie leaned back against the sofa and wrapped her hands around the mug of tea.

Elias raised his brows. "She did?"

"Yes. But now she has to stop. She's determined to be staid and responsible."

"Cristina? What about Mark?"

"What about him?"

"I thought she was supposed to be telling you how wonderful *he* was."

"Oh, yes. She did. They're both going to be staid and responsible."

"Yeah, right."

"Don't be so cynical. You're not giving her much of a chance!"

"It's not my fault she's an impractical airhead."

"No, of course it's not. It's hers. I mean, she's not really an airhead. She's—" Tallie seemed to grope for the suitable word.

Elias waited, wondering what it would be.

Finally Tallie shrugged helplessly. "An airhead," she admitted, stifling a laugh.

And suddenly Elias felt the tension between his shoulders ease. He smiled wryly but felt an odd sort of relief that someone—even Tallie Savas—actually understood.

"But a sweet airhead," Tallie added quickly.

"A sweet airhead who is in my bed. Why? For that matter how?" He certainly hadn't given Cristina a key.

"She got…upset at lunch. We were talking…she *was* talking," Tallie corrected herself, "and she got a little, um…hysterical."

"Hysterical?" The tension came back with a vengeance.

"Pretty much. So I didn't think I ought to leave her there or send her home by herself. So I brought her with me. But having her in the office didn't seem like a very good idea either—"

Elias could believe that. Cristina's behavior had been every bit as bad as he'd feared.

"I considered taking her to my place. But Rosie said I should just bring her up here. To your place. I didn't even know you lived here," she added. "Rosie said she had a key and she got it for me. So I did. It wasn't Cristina's idea," she added firmly. "She said you'd be furious. But, well—" Tallie shrugged "—I didn't give her any choice."

Elias accepted that. He didn't like it—the Cristina part anyway—but he could deal with it. Once he had the whole story, at least. Which he knew he didn't have yet.

"Go on," he said.

Tallie twisted a lock of her hair around her finger. "I was afraid you'd say that." She smiled wryly. "This is the tricky bit."

Elias felt the tension in his neck tighten further.

"I'm not the one who should be telling you this. I shouldn't be involved at all." She stopped and stared at him, as if she could will him to tell her not to go on.

"But you are. So go on," he said implacably.

"Fine. All right." She took a deep breath. "Cristina's pregnant."

*"What!"* So, all right, it was a bellow. He couldn't help it.

Tallie strangled her mug. "Please! Hush. You'll wake her up."

"Damn right I will. *Pregnant?* That idiot! What the hell did she do that for?"

"I gather it wasn't, um, planned."

Elias's jaw clenched. "She can't be that stupid." But evidently she could be. He raked a hand through his hair. "I suppose it's Mark's?" He didn't want to think she might not know.

"It's Mark's. No question."

Apparently Cristina had been at pains to make sure Tallie understood that. But knowing it didn't make Elias much happier. He leaped up and paced around the room, raking his fingers through his hair. "The last thing Cristina needs is a boy toy for the father of her child."

"It would probably be better if you didn't mention that to her," Tallie said mildly.

Elias snorted. "It would be better if the child had any other parents on earth!"

"You don't know that," Tallie argued. "Sometimes parenthood is the making of people."

"Didn't do much for my old man," Elias muttered.

He had never in his life commented on the mathematical impossibility of his own conception having occurred after his parents' wedding day. Still, he shouldn't have mentioned it. "Forget I said that," he muttered, feeling disloyal.

"Of course." Tallie nodded and, thank God, didn't pursue it. "They're getting married."

Elias rolled his eyes. "And that's supposed to make me feel better?"

"I don't think it has much to do with your feelings at all," Tallie said frankly. "You're her brother, not her father or the father of her child."

"I'm the bank," Elias said grimly.

"No, you just run the bank. Or you did," she said reflectively.

Elias's brows snapped down. His gaze met hers. "You think you have more to say about this than I do?"

"No." Tallie shook her head. "I don't think either one of us has anything to say about it ultimately. We can be a stumbling block. Or not."

There was a quiet—but distinct—challenge in her words.

Elias mulled them over. He chewed on the inside of his cheek, trying to come to terms with what she had just told him. It rankled a bit that his sister had confided in Tallie when she hadn't been willing to talk to him.

Of course, Cristina might be an airhead, but she did have some instincts of self-preservation, and there was no doubt she knew what he'd say.

But Tallie was right. The child wasn't his. The decisions weren't his. He rubbed the back of his neck. "So when are they getting married?"

Tallie beamed. "I knew you'd be sensible."

Yeah, well, everyone knew that. When in his life hadn't Elias been sensible? It was what he was, while all the rest of his family went crazy around him. He just stared at her in stony silence.

"They're getting married tomorrow."

"Tomorrow?"

"Well, what point is there in waiting?" Tallie asked. She didn't expect him to answer, though. She went right on. "I told Cristina you'd stand up for them."

"You did *what?*" Elias was appalled.

But Tallie flabbergasted him further by continuing, "I knew you'd want to. It's what you do. You love her. And you take care of your family."

The words were simple, but she made them sound like a truth carved in stone. And then, just when he was about to protest, damned if she didn't reach out and take hold of his hand, squeezing it gently, then hanging on.

Elias stared at her, at her dark eyes so wide and intense, pleading with him. Then he dropped his gaze to her hand wrapped around his, her warm soft fingers curving around his hard cold ones.

He couldn't remember the last time anyone had touched him like that—intensely, personally, honestly. It touched not just his hand, but something deep inside him, stirred it, like a stick stirring the ashes of a nearly dead fire, sparking it, creating embers, heat.

He steeled himself against it.

"I know it's not what you want for her," Tallie went on earnestly, still clutching his hand. "She knows that. She said you have 'high expectations.'"

"I don't ask anyone for anything I wouldn't do myself."

"Of course not." Tallie smiled almost gently. "But Cristina doesn't have the same resiliency you do. Most people don't. Most people wouldn't take on saving a family business when they were, what? Twenty-five years old?"

"Twenty-four. But that's not the point."

"It's part of the point. It speaks to your strength, your determination, your love of your family. What you did by staying on at Antonides when my father foisted me off on you speaks of the same thing," she added with a wry little smile.

Elias scowled. "I love that house," he said, then shrugged. "Besides, it's not a big deal. As a president, you're doing all right." However annoying, it was the truth.

Tallie smiled faintly. "Thanks for the vote of confidence. But this isn't about me. Or about you, really. It's about Cristina and Mark and their child. She wants this child. And she wants to marry Mark. She would have liked for it to have happened differently. But sometimes life just…happens."

"Especially to Cristina," Elias said drily.

Tallie's fingers squeezed his lightly. "Especially to Cristina," she echoed with a smile. "But she's determined to make this work. And from what she told me, that's new to her. Isn't it?"

Slowly, reluctantly, Elias nodded. "But who says she will?"

He had wanted his marriage to work, too, but it hadn't. What he'd wanted hadn't mattered at all.

"Who says she won't?" Tallie countered quietly. "Especially if Mark wants it, too. From everything she said, I gather she has always happily, or not so happily, jumped from one thing to another—"

"And one guy to another," Elias added.

"—her whole life. She never felt any commitment to any of them." Tallie's fingers were massaging his gently, warming them. "She feels commitment to Mark. She loves Mark. And their child."

Elias raised his eyes and looked at her wordlessly. What was there to say? That he didn't believe it? He didn't. But what did he know?

He certainly hadn't known Millicent. If you didn't even know about your own wife or your own marriage—

It was true, what Tallie said about Cristina's lack of previous commitment. She had always had the staying power of a fruit fly. But who knew what anyone else felt, what anyone else was capable of?

"What the hell are my folks going to say?"

"Very little if you support her decision," Tallie predicted. "They'll be upset that she got married so quickly and without them there."

"What do you mean, without them there?"

"Cristina says she doesn't want them there under the circumstances. She says that she and your mother would just battle their way through all the preparations and drive each other crazy and it would be awful. But if it is a done deal—and you support them—then your mother will be fine. Cristina wants it to be fine."

Odd as it seemed, when he thought about it, Elias knew his sister was right. She had their parents pegged. Maybe she did know what she was doing.

"Well, they can't get married tomorrow," he said. "It takes longer than that to get a license, arrange a wedding."

"Mark has already done it."

"How?"

"No idea. When they talked on the phone, Mark said he'd arrange it, and he has. He called a couple of hours ago to say it was all set up for two o'clock tomorrow afternoon in some judge's chambers in Manhattan."

"We have a meeting with Corbett tomorrow at two."

Tallie just looked at him. "Elias." There was gentle reproach tone in her voice.

His mouth twisted, but before he could say anything else, the door buzzer sounded.

"Mark," Tallie predicted.

Elias's hand turned into a fist. "I'd like to punch his lights out."

Tallie curved her fingers around his fist. "I know." She gave it a gentle, knowing squeeze, then she let go of his hand and struggled to get to her feet. "But you won't," she concluded with more confidence in him than he had himself.

"I—"

"You answer the door. I'll wake Cristina."

The buzzer sounded again, short, sharp, impatient.

Elias gritted his teeth and stalked toward the door.

Mark Batakis looked very much as if he expected the punch Elias so desperately wanted to throw. An inch or so shorter than Elias, he was stockier, with dark hair and a nose that had obviously been punched in the past—though not, Elias hoped, for the same reason he wanted to.

"Go ahead," Mark said, reading his body language if not his mind. He thrust out his chin. "Hit me. Do whatever you want, but it isn't going to change anything. I'm still marrying your sister."

"So I hear." Elias stood aside and let the other man enter, then shut the door with a decided click. "So I'll save it—and give it to you later if you ever dare to hurt her."

Mark looked surprised at the reprieve, but no less determined. "I won't hurt her. I love her. Where is she?" He was looking around the dimly lit room with increasing apprehension. "Tina! Tina! What have you done to her?"

"*I*—" Elias's voice was icy "—haven't done anything to her."

The door to the bedroom flew open. "Here I am!" And Cristina ran tearfully into Mark's arms, which folded protectively around her. High drama all around. Elias winced, remembering how Millicent had hated the emotional intensity of Antonides family life.

She'd always found Cristina's outbursts annoying, his father's jovial backslapping irritating, his mother's hugs stifling.

"I'm just not like that, Elias," she'd said more than once. "It's uncomfortable."

But Tallie didn't seem uncomfortable. She went right up to the tearful couple and held out her hand to Mark. "I'm Tallie Savas. I spoke with you earlier. I'm glad to meet you."

And Tallie's matter-of-factness seemed to spark an answering chord in his loony sister. As Elias watched, dumbfounded, Cristina dried her tears and mustered the social skills that their mother had despaired of ever teaching her, introducing Tallie to Mark and vice versa.

She even told Mark how wonderful Tallie had been to her— to them, she corrected herself, giving Tallie a watery smile. Mark heartily agreed, shaking Tallie's hand, thanking her profusely.

"Don't thank me," Tallie said. "I was just doing what Elias would have done if he'd been here."

While none of them believed this for a minute, they were all apparently—even Cristina—on their best behavior and too polite to say so. In the awkward silence that followed Tallie's announcement, however, Cristina took Mark's hand and drew him over to where they could stand facing Elias together.

"I know you knew each other at Yale," she said. "And I know you might not have been friends. But this is different. This is family. This is my brother," she said to Mark, her voice a little wavery but determined. She swallowed, then turned an equally determined look on Elias. "Elias, I want you to meet—and welcome—Mark. My fiancé." There was more than a little defiance in her tone.

Before Elias could do more than grit his teeth, he felt something brush against his shirtsleeve and realized that Tallie had come to stand next to him. For moral support or to step on his foot if he misspoke? Probably the latter.

No matter. No one had ever done it before. He let out a deep breath and stuck out his hand to shake Mark's.

"Congratulations," he said, his voice a little rough.

Mark blinked his surprise, then a grin spread across his face and he gave Elias's hand a strong firm shake. "Thanks. You don't have to worry. I'll take care of your sister," he vowed. "And our child. All our children," he added. "I mean that."

All? Good God. There were going to be more? Elias suppressed a shudder at the thought of a horde of little Cristinas. But she was looking at him with such teary-eyed happiness that he managed an answering smile.

"See that you do," he said evenly to Mark, "and there will never be any problem."

"I'm sure he will." Tallie's voice was firm and cheerful, defusing the gunfighters-at-noon feel to the moment. "Why don't you tell Elias what the plans are so he can arrange to meet you tomorrow?" she suggested to Mark.

Briefly Mark did. What it amounted to was that Elias was expected to wear a dark suit, show up at the judge's chambers, witness the deed and sign the paper afterward. In other words, not a lot.

"And this is all right with you?" Elias asked his sister doubtfully. As weddings went, this was so spare it bore no resemblance to those she'd prattled on about in her girlish dreams.

But Cristina just nodded her head. "It's fine."

"And the parents?"

She bit her lip. "If they would come and not try to argue or run things or make me cry, I would ask them to be there," she said, meeting his gaze. "You know they won't."

Elias nodded. "All right," he said. "I'll be there tomorrow a little before two."

Cristina threw her arms around him and pressed a kiss to his cheek. "Oh, I love you, Elias. You're the best brother in the whole world."

"I'm glad you finally realize that," he said drily. Then because, damn it, he did care, he gave her a hard squeeze in return, then let her loose and said gruffly, "Go home, Cristina,"

Giggling she gave his cheek another kiss. "I will. Don't be a grouch, Eli. Someday I hope you're as happy as I am."

"God forbid."

"You will be," she prophesied. "Just because that witch—"

"Cristina," he said sharply, "go home."

"I'm going," she said. Then, smiling, she hooked her arm in Mark's. "Let's go, darling." Then she turned back to Tallie. "Thank you, Tallie, for everything. You are the best."

"I'm glad you think so."

Mark looped an arm protectively around Cristina, opened the door, then stopped and looked back at Tallie. "Can we give you a lift home?"

"I—"

"I'll see that she gets home," Elias cut in.

Cristina's eyes got wide and round as dinner plates as she looked from him to Tallie and back again, then opened her mouth to stick her foot in it.

"Good night, Cristina," Elias said firmly before she could. "I'll see you tomorrow for your wedding." There was a finality to his tone that even his clueless sister seemed to recognize.

She nodded and blinked rapidly, her mascara sliding further down her cheeks as she smiled tremulously. "Good night. Thank you. Thank you both."

Then at last the door shut behind them.

And there was suddenly such complete silence that Elias thought he could hear his heart beat. Or maybe that was Tallie's.

She was still standing right next to him, close enough that their arms brushed. Close enough for him to make just a half turn to his left to come nearly mouth to nose with her. Close enough to remember all too vividly what it had felt like to be this close…to be even closer. To touch her lips with his.

And all thoughts he'd been trying not to think since Friday night came back with a vengeance as Tallie seemed almost to sway toward him.

It was the crutches, of course. She had no balance. But God, she had beautiful lips. Kissable lips.

Desperately he cleared his throat, tried to find his voice—and his equilibrium. "Thank you… for…for taking care of Cristina." He tried to sound calm and collected. He sounded rusty and out of breath.

"I was glad to do it." There was a huskiness in her voice, as well. Their gazes locked.

It was just like last Friday—only worse. Because this time there were no pain killers involved. There was no baklava.

There was only desire.

It was insane. A mistake. A very bad idea. All of the above.

He should put her in a taxi and see her home, because Tallie Savas was a complication he didn't need in his life. He knew that. If it wasn't smart, it wasn't sensible, it wasn't in the best interests of Antonides Marine or the Antonides family, Elias didn't do it.

For the first time in his adult life Elias didn't give a damn about Antonides Marine or the rest of the Antonides family. He didn't give a damn about being sane and sensible.

Just once…just one damn time, he was going to live for the moment, in the moment.

"To hell with it," he muttered.

He took Tallie's crutches and tossed them aside.

"Elias!"

He shook his head and wrapped his arms around her, drew her close, reveling in the slender curves and softness that seemed to fit so well against him. And then he bent his head and kissed Tallie Savas for all he was worth. His lips found hers and they melted together.

# CHAPTER EIGHT

IT DIDN'T stop at kissing.

Tallie was glad about that.

She told herself she would regret it someday. But even as she tried to form those negative words in her head, she was on her way to the bedroom in Elias's arms, and what her mind was really saying was, "Yes, yes, yes."

Or were those her lips?

No, they were busy nuzzling his neck, kissing his jawline, learning the feel of the rough stubble one way and the silky softness the other. And then he was bending to lay her on his bed. She settled in, snuggled down, raised her hands toward him.

But he didn't drop down beside her. Instead Elias braced himself, hands on the duvet on either side of her arms, and looked down at her, his eyes hooded, his handsome face taut.

"This isn't sensible," he muttered.

Tallie shook her head. "No."

It was possibly the most senseless thing she'd done in her life. He was not Brian. He didn't love her the way Brian had. But this wasn't about love.

It was about coming back to life—feeling something again, wanting something…*someone*—again.

Just that.

She knew he felt the same way. She knew more about his demons now. This afternoon at lunch Cristina had explained why Elias was going to be so upset with her marrying Mark.

"He thinks marriages don't work. He was married," she'd gone on to explain, "to the world's biggest bitch. We called her 'the ice maiden.' She was grasping and demanding and she hated all of us. She wanted Elias—and Antonides Marine. And when it turned out the company had problems and Elias had to spend most of his life fixing them, she walked out!"

Cristina's eyes had flashed with anger. "He doesn't trust anyone now. He doesn't believe in happy endings. He doesn't believe in love."

Tallie believed in love. She'd had it with Brian. She didn't expect to ever have it like that again. She'd been in her own "ice chest" since his death.

But just recently the ice had begun to thaw. Not the emotional ice that held her heart. But the physical ice. At least her hormones were alive and well—and attracted to Elias. His looks, of course, were memorable. His body was hard and muscular. He was one gorgeous specimen of manhood.

But it was more than his looks or his physical attributes that attracted her. It was his energy, his determination, his dynamism. And his kindness to his family. How often had she seen him stop his work to deal with a family problem. He'd done it again today with Cristina.

And on Friday, taking her home, staying all night, nobly refusing what she had so eagerly offered, he had been kind to her.

Elias Antonides was a good man. And he came in a package that was, on every level, too tempting to resist.

She'd tried. God knew she'd done everything she could. She'd turned her back. She'd walked away. She'd dated Martin.

Suddenly she laughed. Her father had always told her never to turn her back on her problems. "It doesn't work," he said. "They always come back and bite you on the ass."

Elias had been nibbling her jaw, her neck her shoulders. Was he working his way south?

"Something funny?" he growled, lifting his head and noting her smile. His face was taut, his body was hard. She could feel tremors running through him where her hands pressed against his back.

"A little. I was thinking of something my father always said."

"Your father?" Elias pulled back abruptly. His eyes were glazed and he looked somewhere between pleasure and pain. But he was clearly aghast at the direction of her thoughts. A muscle jumped in his jaw. "You're thinking about *your father?*"

Tallie kissed the spot where the muscle was twitching. "Just for a moment." And while she often told her father when his advice was particularly apropos, she didn't think she'd mention this instance.

"Forget him," she muttered. And before Elias could pull back completely, she pulled Elias's head down and began kissing him again.

He resisted for only a moment, and then he came down beside her, as hungry and desperate and eager as she was. And Tallie welcomed him with open arms. She fumbled with the buttons of his shirt, wanting desperately to get her hands inside it, to run her fingers over his hot skin.

He didn't bother with her buttons, just tugged her top out of her trousers and slid his hands up under it. His fingers were callused, slightly rough. Working-man's hands. She'd noticed it before and had wondered how a man who ran a business got work-roughened hands.

Cristina had explained that he'd done most of the renovations on the building and all of them in his apartment. He had made those beautiful cabinets in the kitchen, that stunning bar between it and the living room.

He had talented hands. Good with wood—and good with her. They felt wonderful, made her skin tingle wherever they touched. Made her shiver with longing to have them touch her more.

She got his shirt undone, and he levered himself up enough to strip it off, then reached down and peeled hers off as well. Then he bent his head and began kissing her bare shoulders, her breasts, and Tallie shivered.

"Are you cold?" Elias's voice was muffled against her.

She shook her head. "Burning." She threaded her hands through his thick hair, then slid them down across his shoulders and traced the line of his spine. His back was smooth and hard with muscles. She spread her palms against them, kissed his shoulders, his jaw, his chin.

And then once more he captured her mouth with his and rolled her over so she lay on top of him. Deftly he reached behind her and unhooked her bra. And as it fell away, he cupped her breasts in his hands, lifted his head and kissed each one in turn, laved it softly with his tongue, made her shiver and grip his shoulders, tense with longing for him.

"Elias!" His name hissed between her teeth.

He lay back against the pillow and smiled up at her, watching her beneath hooded lids all the while that his fingers tracing patterns lightly on her sensitive skin, swirling over her breasts and down across her abdomen.

Mesmerized, Tallie held perfectly still, savoring the feel of them, their soft rough touch gliding over her skin, leaving fiery trails of longing in their wake. The fire built, grew hotter and more intense. And then he flicked open the button to her slacks and drew her zip down.

As his hands parted the fabric, instinctively Tallie rose up on her knees. He pushed the trousers down on her hips, then slid his fingers inside to delve beneath her silky panties and found her hot and wet and wanting. He touched her there.

A breath hissed through Tallie's teeth. She bit her lip and pressed against his questing fingers, whimpering as he stroked and rubbed and lifted his head to kiss her breasts, to take first one nipple and then the other in his mouth until she couldn't resist. Her body tensed and trembled, desperate, needy, aching.

It had been so long.

And yet she wasn't ready, resisted taking the release he offered. No! Not now. Not yet.

Deliberately she rolled to his side, but not away, wanting more—wanting him—and determined that, hungry as they were, they were nowhere close to finished yet. He had made her burn for him. Now it was her turn.

She pressed kisses to his arm, to his shoulder, then raised up on one elbow to lean over and kiss his chest. He watched her, his dark eyes hooded, skin taut across his cheekbones. She smiled and drew squiggles over his chest with her fingers and lazy circles with her tongue. The breath hissed out between his teeth, and he tensed beneath her touch as she had under his.

"Tallie," he muttered, his fingers knotting in the duvet.

"Mmm? Want something?"

"You."

"You've got me." Lifting her head, she looked into his eyes and smiled. His own smile was strained, his breathing shallow. She stopped tracing with her fingers and walked them slowly down his chest and his hard belly to his belt. She undid it, then eased down the zip and bent her head to kiss the line of dark hair that disappeared beneath his boxers.

Elias jerked at the touch of her mouth. "Tallie!"

She didn't answer, just moved her head back and forth, brushing her hair against his belly. Then she slipped her hand beneath the elastic and felt hot, hard, straining flesh meet her fingers there. She curved her fingers around him, weighed and stroked his length. His hips arched. A sharp breath hissed between his lips. "Stop! Just…wait."

Tallie waited. She bent her head and kissed him lightly on the chest, then smoothed her hand up his body to feel his heart hammering beneath her fingers. Hammering for her. Wanting her.

Wordlessly Elias reached up and grasped her fingers and drew them to his lips, kissed them one after another, nibbled them, tasted them, heated her blood all over again.

And then he pulled her down against him and rolled them over. And somehow they managed to shed the rest of their clothes, no mean trick as it entailed getting her slacks down over her cast. But Elias did it. He was gentle but efficient as he worked her trouser leg down over the cast.

"Amazing. You're good at everything," Tallie murmured.

He grinned crookedly. "Glad you think so," he said, his voice ragged. And then he pressed a kiss to her knee above the cast and then to her toes as he slid the trouser leg over them. It nearly un-did her.

And then he was sheathing himself to protect her, and she smiled again because it was so like Elias to, without a word, take the responsibility.

He caught her gaze. "What?"

She shook her head and held out her arms to him. And he came to her, settling between her thighs, eager now, pressing against her.

And Tallie reached for him, drew him down and in. It was as close as two people could be. And when he began to move, in-stinctively she moved with him, dug her fingers into his back, urged him closer, deeper, harder. Until he shattered and she shat-tered with him. And they were no longer separate.

They were one.

She hadn't expected that. That was how she had felt with Brian—as if their bodies, their hearts, their souls had merged.

She had been so lonely, so empty without him. And yet she'd grown accustomed to it, had—over the years—even taken ref-uge in her loneliness. It was safer than loving. Safer than caring.

She was very much afraid she was beginning to care about Elias Antonides.

And that wasn't safe—or sensible—at all.


It hadn't done the trick.

He'd made love with Tallie Savas to get her out of his system. To stop thinking about her. To stop closing his eyes and seeing her even then. To stop *wanting* her every minute of the day....

And within moments of having had her—of having been *in-side* her—he had wanted to be there again.

They'd rested, they'd murmured, they'd touched, they'd stroked. And then he'd had her again. And she'd had him.

And still it hadn't been enough.

Making love with Tallie hadn't assuaged his desire. It had heightened it. Sharing intimacies with her had only whetted his appetite for more. He wanted to make her crazy. He wanted to feel her body respond to his. He wanted to feel her nails digging into his flesh as her body climaxed and shuddered beneath him. He wanted her over him, riding him. He wanted to wrap his fingers in her hair and bury his face against her neck and slide right back into the closest he'd ever felt to being whole.

And at the same time he wanted to run a million miles!

Tallie Savas was not for him.

He told himself that over and over all night long. Beyond their reluctant temporary partnership in Antonides Marine—a partnership of necessity—she didn't want a relationship. She was all about business. And so was he.

What the hell was the matter with him?

He'd gone to bed with a fair number of women since Millicent had left, and he'd *never* thought in terms of the future with any of them. The word *relationship* had never entered his mind. While he had always enjoyed the experience, he'd never lain beside a woman and wondered where things were going from here.

Not the way he lay next to Tallie now, wide-awake and staring at the ceiling while she slept soundly and, he hoped, satisfied, in his arms.

That should be enough. They had been attracted, yes. They'd felt an itch and they'd scratched it—very successfully, he reflected. Making love with Tallie Savas had been an exciting mix of give and take, of gentleness and passion. It had been beautiful and mind-blowing all at once.

He'd never experienced anything like it.

Which was probably why he wanted more. More lovemaking; that went without saying. The itch was very definitely still there. But so was this irritating niggling demand for something else. He wanted more...*more*...even as he knew it was a mistake.

It was all Nikos Costanides's fault, he decided.

Seeing Nikos and Mari together, happy, fulfilled, loving had reawakened all those long-buried memories. They had made him want the things he used to want—the things he thought he'd have by now with Millicent.

And because he was physically attracted to Tallie, those longings had simply attached themselves to her.

It was all very logical when he thought about it.

No matter that she was exactly the wrong woman. No matter that he didn't want any woman for more than a night. No matter, no matter, no matter.

Damn it to hell.

It was Cristina's fault, too. While he was passing around blame, she deserved her share. He was going to have to stand there and watch her get married in scant hours. To Mark Batakis, of all people, who raced fast boats, fought at the drop of a hat, could drink his entire college under the table, and had, conservatively, fifty girlfriends during their college years.

But Cristina loved him. And he said he loved her. So that made it all right. Elias snorted derisively.

What the hell did either one of them know about love? If you loved, you left yourself open for being gutted the way he'd been gutted by Millicent. You had hopes and dreams that depended on another person. And they let you down.

There were no numbers to crunch, no balance sheets to check, no projections to consider. There was nothing sensible to base it on. Nothing logical. It was all emotion and desire and *love.* They were idiots!

Tallie must have sensed his unrest, for she turned toward him in her sleep and nestled closer, her lips brushing his bare chest, the fresh scent of her shampoo teasing his nose. It drove him insane with wanting.

But it wasn't love, he assured himself. It was attraction. Lust. Animal passion. A release they had both needed because they had worked so hard, been so consumed with work, with sorting out what to do about Corbett's, with Cristina's little bombshell.

He was sure that was the way Tallie saw it. She certainly wasn't lying awake anguishing over what they'd done, was she?

Of course not.

But he was. And if he didn't get up and get out he was very much afraid he might wake her and do it all over again.

Carefully Elias eased himself out of bed. It was nearly seven. He could shave and shower and be dressed by the time she woke up. It would be easier to be distant and properly businesslike that way.

It was harder, though, than he imagined. *He* was harder. As he stood beneath the shower, he kept remembering his hands on her and hers on him, and he was tempted to go out and wake her, to bring her with him into the shower where he could touch her all over again and—

Damn, didn't this water get any colder?

His teeth were chattering by the time he had shaved and dressed and combed his hair. But at least he had his self-control firmly in place again.

Then he opened the door and confronted the sight of a rumpled and completely bare—except for her purple cast—Tallie easing herself into one of his shirts.

So much for self-control.

So much for cold showers. He'd need a glacier to get over this!

"Oh, good morning." Tallie flashed him a quick smile and continued to do up the buttons. The eager lover she'd been in bed was the breezy CEO now, even wearing his shirt.

"Morning." He hoped his voice wasn't as ragged as it sounded to his own ears.

"Hope you don't mind about the shirt. I just need something to wear until I've washed. I don't suppose you have a hair dryer?" She was talking quickly, papering over the awkwardness, apparently not about to do a postmortem—or postcoital—of the night before.

Not that he wanted to, but—one of the reasons for keeping business and pleasure separate, obviously.

He shook his head. "No hair dryer."

"Can't shower unless I can dry the cast with one," Tallie said ruefully. "How about a washer and dryer?"

"I've got a laundry room off the kitchen."

"Great. Could I throw my stuff in?"

"I'll do it." Much better than standing there looking at her wearing his shirt, wanting to rip it off her and take her back to bed. Swiftly Elias gathered up her clothes—and his—and bolted for the door. He had the laundry going and had just finished making coffee when she came into the kitchen. The shirt hit her above midthigh. He knew what was beneath it.

He cleared his throat. "Cup of coffee?"

"Please."

He poured two. "Bacon? Eggs? Toast? Oatmeal?" He didn't look at her again. A man could only stand so much temptation.

But Tallie was completely blasé. "Toast," she decided. He heard the clatter as she leaned her crutches against the bar, then one of the stools moved as she sat up on it. "Thanks," she said when he set a mug in front of her. "You have a great place here."

He put the bread in the toaster. "I'm working on it."

"Cristina told me. I had no idea you were doing all the work not just here, but in the whole building. I didn't even know you owned it."

He shrugged. "It was a good investment. And I haven't done all of it. I've hired out the wiring and stuff. I do the dirty work—and the wood."

"So you did all this?" She was looking at the kitchen cabinets and running her fingers appreciatively over the bar.

Elias tried not to remember what else her fingers had rubbed over. "I did all the woodwork."

"Then why are you wasting your time at Antonides Marine?"

He frowned and looked at her for the first time since she'd come into the room. "What?"

"I'm sorry. It's not a waste, I guess. It's just…this is beautiful. Way more beautiful than mergers and acquisitions." She stroked the gleaming wood again. "And you obviously love doing it." She smiled, understanding him.

He didn't want her understanding him. It undermined his resolve to keep this casual. He shrugged dismissively. "No time." Besides, he enjoyed the business, too, though admittedly—to himself at least—not as much as he'd enjoyed building boats. Not as much as he still enjoyed working with wood. The toast popped up. He put it on plates and got out butter and jam. "Besides, you can't make a living at it. Here. Help yourself."

Tallie buttered her toast, but she pressed on. "I'll bet you could," she argued. "Lots of people would kill to have something this beautiful in their home."

"Kill, maybe. Pay for? Not likely." Elias shook his head. But they paid Nikos—and paid him well, a little voice inside his head piped up. He shut it down. "It's just a hobby. I have more important things to do."

"Antonides Marine." Tallie said.

"That's right. And don't suggest I leave it all to you," he said sharply, unsure why the conversation made him feel edgier and more exposed than he'd felt naked in bed with her. It was easier to pick a fight with her.

But Tallie didn't oblige him. "You can't, can you?" she pointed out mildly. "Not if you want your house back."

Exactly. It all came back to the house. Last night's intimacy was simply a byproduct of a bloody business deal.

"That's right," he said gruffly. "And I ought to get to it right now." He shot back the cuff of his shirt to glance at his watch. "It's nearly eight. The wash is in there." He jerked his head toward the door to a small utility room off the kitchen. "It should be done in a few minutes. You can put it in the dryer."

He took one last swallow of coffee and felt it churn in his stomach as he set the mug on the counter and then brushed past Tallie to head for the door.

"I didn't intend to be rude, Elias," she said to his back.

He stopped at the door and turned, meeting her gaze, trying to focus on her eyes and not on her delectable body clad only in his shirt. He tried, too, to forget last night and remember that today was all about business. *They* were all about business. "I know that."

"Good." She paused. "And…about last night—" She stopped.

He waited. Didn't breathe.

The colour rose in her cheeks. "It was…um…nice."

"Nice?" He stared at her. *Nice?*

"More than nice," she amended, deeply flushed now, agitated, too. She was strangling her toast. "Thank you."

Christ! What was he supposed to say to that? *Thank you, too?*

"Yeah." He gave a jerky nod. His teeth clenched. He had to consciously relax his jaw, then take a breath and let it out. "Take your time," he said at last. "We can have our meeting about Corbett's whenever you get there."

She flashed him a quick smile. "Thanks. Could you tell Mark I'll be a little late."

"Mark?"

Tallie rolled her eyes. "Your soon-to-be-brother-in-law, Mark."

"I thought the wedding wasn't until two."

"It isn't. So there's no reason he can't work until noon."

"What?" Elias gaped at her, disbelieving his own ears. "You didn't."

Tallie just shrugged happily. "Yes, I did. I hired him."

When she finally got her clothes clean and dried and made it into the office it was half past nine. She could have been a few minutes earlier, but she'd taken a side trip to buy bagels from the shop down the street.

"I was a little busy last night," she apologized to Rosie and Dyson, and hoped her blushes wouldn't betray her and that no one would remember she was wearing the same silk shirt and black trousers she'd had on yesterday—except for the bright pink scarf knotted at her neck. She'd just bought it from the street vendor in front to the bagel shop.

"You don't have to bring something every day," Rosie said even as she peered in the bag. "It's not like we expect it."

"Of course not," Dyson assured her, helping himself to a bagel, slicing it in half and slathering it with cream cheese. "However—" he took an enormous bite, chewed and swallowed, then grinned at her "—it's fine with me if you do."

Tallie grinned, too, then looked around. "Where's Paul?" which wasn't what she wanted to ask, but asking, "Where's Elias? Has he killed Mark yet?" didn't seem like the best question.

In fact, the door was closed to Elias's office and she didn't hear any shouting, which she hoped was a good thing.

Rosie said, "They went to meet a publicist."

Tallie's brows went up. "Publicist?"

Rosie nodded. "Someone Mark knew from his races. Said he thought the guy could do an ad campaign for the pleasure-craft line."

"Really?" It was better than she'd dared hope. After she'd told Elias she'd hired Mark, she'd tried to explain her reasoning.

"Having him work for the company, as long as he's willing, will give Cristina the sense that you accept him, that you have faith in him."

"I'm letting her marry him, damn it!" Elias had snarled.

Not that he could have stopped her, Tallie thought. But she forwent to pointing this out. She'd just nodded. "But this way you show you have confidence in him."

"And not that I just want to keep an eye on him?" Elias raised a brow.

Tallie had smiled. "Well, that, too," she agreed. "But he has things to offer. He's a racer. A proven winner."

"A playboy."

"A man who's attractive to women," she'd corrected.

"Who's marrying my sister," Elias retorted through his teeth.

"Who is in love and wants to spend the rest of his life with one woman. It's very romantic," Tallie revised.

Elias had given her a hard look.

"Look, we have a speedboat division in the pleasure-craft side. It's basic, not the luxury stuff your dad was doing. But it's there. And it's pretty stagnant from what I can see. It can be developed. It *should* be developed. Mark's handsome. Charming—"

Elias had contributed a couple more unprintable adjectives or two which Tallie determinedly ignored.

"—and he could be an excellent spokesman. It's worth considering."

He had grunted and left, unconvinced.

But apparently, against all odds, Mark had convinced him. It was cause for hope. And Elias not being there made it easier to get through the morning.

She wasn't used to waking up in mens' apartments. For that

matter, she wasn't used to going to bed with them. She hadn't made love with anyone but Brian. She'd almost resigned herself to never sleeping with anyone again.

And now she had.

With Elias Antonides of all people.

Undoubtedly a colossal mistake. She'd mixed business and pleasure. She'd slept with a man who clearly didn't want a relationship. And even knowing that, she knew she would do it again.

Was this how affairs started?

Tallie had never seen herself as the sort who had affairs. But probably, she thought honestly, most women didn't. They found themselves in situations and they *responded.* The way she had responded to Elias last night. The way she would probably respond if he walked into her office right now.

So it was a shock when there was a brisk rap on the door and before she could do more than look up a black-haired pirate strode in.

"Theo?" She stared, astonished and then delighted at the sight of her oldest brother. "Theo!" She leapt out of her chair, forgetting her cast, and nearly fell over the desk. Righting herself she waited for him to come to her. "What are you doing here?"

It had been months since she'd seen him. Theo Savas was as footloose as their father was tied down.

He kicked the door shut and crossed the room to haul her into his arms and give her a hug. "On my way to Newport. Testing a new boat there. Sailing her to Spain if I decide she's good. I called the old man from the airport but he was out wheeling and dealing, so I asked for you. Figured you might have finally wormed your way into the company."

"Not quite." Tallie smiled ruefully and shook her head.

"His secretary told me you were here." Theo frowned. "What the hell are you doing here of all places?" Then he glanced down, spotted her cast and demanded, "And what have you done to yourself now?"

"Lost a crosswalk to a truck?"

Theo looked at her, appalled. "You could have been killed!" It jolted how much he sounded like Elias.

"Well, I wasn't. Come sit down. I'll get some coffee. Tell me what you're doing here. You hate the city."

She would have gone down the hall, but Theo picked up her phone and asked Rosie to please bring some in. Then he hung up and caught the surprise on Tallie's face, and shrugged. "It's her job. She works for you," he said.

"I know that, but—when did you get so corporate?"

Theo grinned. "I can delegate when I have to. I don't haul all those sails myself." He waited for her to sit down, then dropped into one of the chairs and regarded the skyscrapers of Manhattan across the river. "Hell of a view, Tal."

"I owe it all to you."

"Me?" He raised a quizzical brow.

"My job. You won a boat race," she reminded him, "against Aeolus Antonides. For which you won a house…for the moment, anyway, and I got to be president of Antonides Marine."

"The son of a gun got you a presidency?" Theo shook his head, amazed. Then his mouth twisted. "Well, something good came out of it, anyway."

"You won the race," Tallie reminded him.

"Yeah."

She expected him to grin, relishing his triumph. But he just looked grim.

"Something wrong with that?" she asked. She was used to Theo looking a bit ragged and tired. The sea and the sun did that to a man. But she could see now that he looked agitated, too.

"Should've thrown it," he said unexpectedly. "Wish I'd never seen the damn thing."

"What thing?"

"The house on Santorini."

Tallie's eyes widened. "You've been there?"

Theo raked a hand through unruly black hair. "Yeah."

"I, um, thought it was supposed to be beautiful. Elias, the managing director, Elias Antonides," she clarified, doing her best to sound professional, "says his family is very fond of it."

"They are." Theo's voice was grim. He stood abruptly and began pacing the confines of her office like a panther trapped in a suitcase.

Tallie watched, fascinated. Theo was, except when it came to sailing, the most easygoing of men. She'd never seen anything ruffle Theo—not even her overbearing father—but something was definitely ruffling Theo now.

There was a tap on the door and Rosie appeared with coffee and bagels. She set the tray on the desk. And while she was doing it, she took a long and appreciative look at Theo. All women did.

And ordinarily Theo returned the compliment. Today, though, Theo just scowled out the window, not paying the least bit of attention. Rosie sighed and left, shutting the door behind her.

Tallie went back to the subject at hand. "What's wrong with the house?"

"Not what," Theo snapped. "Who!"

"Like there's a ghost in it?"

"Don't be an idiot!" Theo cracked his knuckles. "There's no ghost. There's a girl."

"You mean, like, a little girl?"

Maybe the housekeeper had a pesky daughter. Tallie could envision—remotely—a five-year-old would be impervious to Theo's charms. But it wouldn't last. And she didn't imagine a five-year-old would be living there alone.

Theo glared. "No, I don't mean a little girl."

"Well then," Tallie grinned, "you certainly ought to be able to handle her. Use the legendary Savas charm."

Theo snorted. He cracked his knuckles again. He paced.

Tallie was curious beyond belief. "Don't tell me she's impervious." She giggled at her brother's discomfiture. "Come on, Theo. Tell all!"

"No. It doesn't matter. Besides, when I get back she'll be gone." He turned to stare out across the river, shoulders hunched. "She damned well better be," he muttered more to himself than to her.

Tallie had often studied Theo's back as he'd stood onboard a sailboat staring out at the horizon. She'd always thought how strong and determined he looked, the captain of his ship, master of his destiny.

Today she thought he looked as if he were about to walk the plank.

It was not easy to contemplate. Theo, as the oldest of her brothers, had always been her protector, not teasers and tormenters, like Yiannis, Demetrios and George. She had hero worshiped Theo since she'd been old enough to trail around after him. He had always had the answer to all the world's problems—or he had been able to assure her that the problem she was obsessing about didn't really matter.

And now?

"Are you okay, Theo?" she asked him, concerned now.

"Swell." He flung himself back down in the chair and stared morosely at his hands.

"No," Tallie decided. "You're not. You need to do something fun."

Theo dragged his palms down his face. "What I need is to sleep. I've had a hell of a week. I just got off a plane from Athens. I've got to pick up a car to drive to Newport tonight so I can meet a crew there and test a new boat."

"Okay. You can take a nap at my place," Tallie decided, "and then we'll figure things out from there."

It was the distraction she needed. Elias was going to Cristina and Mark's wedding this afternoon. She was not. She had declined when Cristina had invited her, saying that she didn't think it was a good idea. And that was *before* she'd slept with Elias.

Thank God, she'd had a little bit of sense.

"Come on," she said to her brother and led the way down the hall. "We're going out for a while," she told Rosie.

Rosie nodded and eyed Theo again, then grinned broadly and said, "Have fun," in a knowing way.

This time Theo flashed his dimples and his grin and winked. "We will."

While Theo slept—or tried to—she baked a poppy seed cake and *kolaches* to take into work tomorrow. And while she baked, she made every effort to think about something other than Elias, which was well-nigh impossible.

It was a relief when Theo finally got up. He still looked tired and distracted. But any questions from her just made him scowl and tell her to mind her own business.

After being told that, she didn't much feel like asking his advice about hers. Besides, if Theo couldn't handle his relationships, which were far less complicated than hers, she could hardly expect him to help her figure things out.

She did ask him what he did to clear his head, though.

"Go sailing," he said promptly.

"No boat," she said just as promptly.

"Or sometimes, when I can't sail, I run."

Tallie looked at the cast on her ankle and sighed. "Well, that's out, too."

"What's the problem?" Theo was perched on a bar stool in her kitchen, eating a *kolache,* but studying her intently at the same time.

Aware of his scrutiny, Tallie turned away and concentrated on drying the dishes. "Nothing much. I'm all right." She shrugged lightly. "Just trying to figure things out. You know, new job and all."

Theo grinned. "You're the president now. You can do what you want."

"If only it were that simple."

"Old Man Antonides giving you problems?"

"Not really. He was a figurehead. His son runs—ran—" She shut her mouth.

"*He's* giving you trouble?" Theo looked as if he might punch Elias out.

"No, not really," Tallie said quickly. "We get along pretty, um, well now. It's just…complicated." And it was making her cheeks burn.

Theo looked at her narrowly. "Complicated how?"

"Never mind." She finished drying the dishes and hung the towel neatly on the rack with far more attention to getting its corners square than was entirely necessary.

When she turned back, Theo was still staring at her. Tallie met his gaze defiantly.

He looked away first. But his mouth twisted and he shook his head.

"We need a boat," he decided. "Let's go get some fresh air. But, kid, I'll tell you one thing—the old man has a lot to answer for."

Theo, being Theo, found a boat—not a sailboat, of course. But he took her rowing in Central Park.

It was the best he could do, he said ruefully, on short notice.

Tallie had never been rowing in Central Park. She nearly fell into the water trying to negotiate the dock and the tipping boat with the cast on her leg. But once she got in and settled, sitting there in the boat while Theo rowed them over the water was surprisingly soothing. With the late afternoon sun on her face, the blue sky overhead and the traffic and noise of the city at a distance, she felt calmer, more in control.

The emotion generated by her night with Elias seemed less acute. The problem, she could see now, was coming to terms with her expectations.

She had no right to expectations. They were two consenting adults who had shared a night of intimacy. And yes, she liked him. She wouldn't have gone to bed with him if she hadn't.

But she could deal with it. She wasn't going to throw herself at him—or off a bridge—no matter what. She was simply grateful to him for waking her up again, for making her feel alive again.

He had proved to her that there was life after Brian. She would find it. She was determined now to find it.

It just wouldn't be with him.

The realization settled her down. She caught Theo's eye and smiled across at him. "You're right. It helps."

"Does it?" he said wryly.

And then each of them went back to their own thoughts without a word being spoken.

They spent an hour on the small lake, then they had dinner at a little German place in Yorkville, and finally she accompanied him to pick up the hired car he'd arranged to drive out to Newport.

"I'll take you home on my way," he told her.

"No. You go on. It's a long drive. You don't need to mess with Brooklyn traffic, too." He looked as though he would have argued, but Tallie insisted. "I'll get a cab. Don't worry. And thank you. It was fun." She gave him a kiss and got a bone-crushing hug in return.

"Take care of yourself. Don't do anything I wouldn't do." Theo winked at her.

Tallie laughed. "License for everything, in other words." But she was all right now. Steady, balanced, sensible.

She had her equilibrium back—until the elevator door opened in front of her apartment and she saw Elias standing there.

# CHAPTER NINE

"WHERE the hell have you been?"

It wasn't the way to start the conversation. Elias knew that. But it was nearly ten o'clock, for God's sake. She'd been gone for hours.

According to Dyson and the temp—Laura or Cora or something—who were still in the office when Elias came in from putting Cristina and bloody Mark on a plane to Bermuda, Tallie had left with a man in the middle of the afternoon.

"What man?" he'd demanded. "You mean Martin?"

The temp had giggled. "Oh, no. A real man."

"Not Martin," Dyson had concurred. "Some dark-haired stud. I didn't talk to him."

What stud?

Dyson hadn't known. "Never seen him before."

And there was no one else around to ask.

Not that it was any of his business, of course. Tallie had every right to go out with any stud she wanted.

But not in the middle of the day. Not when she was supposed to be working, being the bloody president of Antonides Marine! If she wasn't going to do her job, she ought to be fired.

When he'd stomped up to his apartment, he'd called her to find out, in an offhand way, what exactly was going on. But all he'd got was her answering machine.

Five times!

He had gone back down to the office to get her cell phone number from Rosie's phone book. But her cell phone was switched off.

Where the hell was the consummate businesswoman now?

Was she all right? he worried, concerned for her welfare. That was what sent him round to her apartment. He'd just wanted to make sure she was all right, that she hadn't been attacked by any dark-haired studly stranger.

But she wasn't there.

So he waited. And waited. For two damn hours—all the while imagining the worst!

And now here she was, looking wild and windblown, sunburned and gorgeous. Not to mention astonished to see him.

"Elias?"

"No, the big bad wolf," he snarled. "Where have you been? Dyson said you left the office in the middle of the afternoon!"

"I told Rosie. Was there a problem?" She looked genuinely concerned as she fumbled to get her key out of her purse.

Elias's jaw bunched. "There damned well could have been."

She stopped and looked at him. "But there wasn't?"

"No." He clipped off the word. He knew he was making way too much out of this. "So, who was the stud?"

Tallie goggled. "Stud?"

Elias's teeth ground together. "The dark-haired stud—to quote Laura the temp—that you ran off with."

Tallie laughed. "Maura," she corrected him. "Her name is Maura."

He didn't care if her name was Rumplestiltskin, damn it! *"Who was he?"*

Tallie turned the key in the lock and pushed open the door. "Theo," she said. "My brother."

"Theo?" He didn't understand why his knees suddenly wobbled. *"Your brother?"*

"Yes He was on his way to Newport. From Athens. Apparently he was at your house in Santorini." Tallie said this last as if she were reluctant to admit it, but Elias didn't give a damn about that. He didn't give a damn about anything other than that the dark-haired stud was her *brother*.

"Some girl there was giving him fits."

"Girl?" Elias echoed vaguely.

Tallie shrugged. "I don't know anything more than that. He muttered a bunch of stuff about a girl, but he wouldn't say any more. Maybe she lives in the village?"

"Maybe." Who cared? Not him. He followed her into her apartment. She looked a little surprised, a little curious, a little wary. She kicked off her shoes and tossed her bag on the little table next to the door. "Do you know her?" she asked.

"No."

She didn't matter. The only woman that mattered right now was standing across the room from him. Elias shut the door and leaned against it, just watching her, wanting her.

"Well, I don't know anything else," Tallie went on, talking rapidly. "Theo's my best brother, but he can be disgustingly closemouthed about things. I was just glad to see him. It's been ages. He was exhausted. So we came back here so he could grab a nap. I wasn't getting anything d—" She stopped abruptly and began again. "I came, too, because my ankle was aching. And…why are you leaning against the door?"

Because it seemed like a better idea than walking across the room, ripping her clothes off and having his way with her. But the minute he thought it, he knew he was wrong. There was no better idea than making love to Tallie.

"I'm not," he said, and pushed away from the door, strode across the room and swept her into his arms.

It was the first thing that had felt right all day.

"Elias!" She stiffened for just a moment, then melted into his embrace. She wrapped her arms around, hanging on to him, holding him close as her lips met his.

Kissing Tallie, touching Tallie, burying his face in her hair, breathing in the scent of her—it was heady and exhilarating and, oddly, like coming home, the more so because he'd spent the whole day dealing with things he'd rather not have dealt with—

like Mark and Cristina—and the last two hours imagining the worst about Tallie and her dark-haired stud.

And now she was here. In his arms. He was kissing her.

And she was kissing him in return.

She seemed just as eager, just as desperate as he was, pulling his shirttails out, sliding her hands up beneath it, stroking his hot skin, even as he was doing the same to her. Buttons popped; zippers slid.

"Tallie!"

"Mmm?"

"We're not going to make it to the bed if you— Tal!" His voice strangled as he sought to keep control.

She stopped. Took her hands off him, holding them up in the air like some bank robber under the sheriff's gun. Oh, God. He couldn't think and make love to Tallie Savas at the same time!

So who needed to think?

He scooped her up into his arms and staggered into her bedroom where he lowered her to the bed.

"Now, where were we?" she mused, smiling up at him. "Ah, yes, I remember." And then her hands began their feverish work again.

"Jeez, Tallie!" But it was exquisite what she was doing to him. Desperate for more, he slid between her thighs and into the warmth of her. And that place was the most right of all.

And then it was his turn to stop, to shake his head no when she urged him on. "I want," he said through his teeth, "to make…it last."

"Why?"

"Why?" Her question confounded him.

A smile touched her lips and she gave a little wriggle against the sheets. "The sooner you get started, the sooner we can do it all again!" She shrugged and looked at him hopefully. "Just trying to be logical."

Far be it from him to defy logic.

And when she kissed him again and urged him to respond, he knew he didn't need any urging at all.

"Whatever you say," he muttered. Then he bent his head and

kissed her again, long and deep and hard, as if he could imprint himself on her memory, as if he could brand her and make her his alone. And then he began to move.

He didn't make it last. He shattered in moments. So did Tallie, whispering his name as she arched into his final thrust. And then they lay, spent, still wrapped in each other's arms.

And still it wasn't enough.

He'd just had her—and he wanted her all over again.

"They're married! My baby is married! Cristina is married, Elias!" His mother's voice bleated in his ear, increasingly more shrill with every sentence.

And good morning to you, too, he thought wearily. She was not the first person he wanted to hear from today.

He wanted Tallie to breeze into his office and tempt him with some bakery confection—or something else. But that wasn't going to happen. She'd breezed in to the office, all right. She'd even brought some *kolaches* she'd made yesterday. But she had on her President Tallie hat. She was charming and friendly—and totally professional.

Which meant, he supposed, that they were having an affair: passionate, torrid sex at night, business as usual during the day.

He wouldn't have wanted it any other way, of course.

But still…

"Elias! Did you hear me?" His mother demanded.

"Yes, Ma. I know," he said now, regretting that he had allowed Rosie to put the call through in the first place. But it had seemed smarter to get it over with before his mother had a chance to work up to full-blown hysteria.

He had insisted yesterday, before he'd put them on the plane, that Cristina call their parents at once and tell them about the wedding.

"When we're in Bermuda," she'd promised. "I'll call them tomorrow. I want my wedding night without angst, Elias," she said firmly.

And he hadn't been able to argue with that.

She had obviously called bright and early this morning and given their parents the news. And just as obviously, whatever she'd said, it hadn't been enough, and he was going to have to do mop-up work. As usual.

"You were there," Helena accused. "She said you were invited!"

"They needed a witness."

"I would have witnessed!" Helena wailed. "Why didn't you tell me?" Elias had to hold the phone away from his ear.

"Because it wasn't my wedding, Ma," he said. "It wasn't my decision."

"Since when do you let your sister make foolish decisions."

"It's her life."

"You should have told me anyway. What sort of mother doesn't go to her own daughter's wedding?"

"One who doesn't know her daughter is getting married," Elias said logically.

"She didn't even have a dress. I suppose she got married in some tacky spandex and combat boots." Helena's complaint was somewhere between a question and an accusation.

"She looked fine," Elias said. "She had a dress."

"What sort of dress?"

He tried to remember. But he hadn't been thinking about his sister. He'd been thinking about Tallie, who should damned well have been there witnessing the wedding with him. After all, it was her fault Mark now had a job in the firm and was part of his family.

And Cristina's dress? He couldn't remember much.

"I think it was purple," he ventured.

"*Purple?*" Helena invariably lapsed into Greek when the stakes were high. She lapsed now, rattling on furiously, making it sound as if the fashion police would arrest Cristina the moment she set foot again on New York soil.

"She looked great," Elias cut in. "And it was her wedding, so it was her choice. Mark liked it."

God knew why he was going out of his way to defend his sister. He had no great hopes that the marriage would last. But the deed was done. And he had to admit that Cristina looked more determined than he had ever seen her. And Mark had said his vows with a firmness that had surprised Elias.

Of course, a ceremony did not a marriage make, as he well knew.

"I should have been there," his mother muttered.

"You can be there for the baby."

"*Baby?* What baby?"

Oh, hell. He'd forgotten she didn't know about that.

"Well, of course there will be a baby eventually," he said hastily. "They're bound to have one. Cristina loves kids. So does Mark," he improvised. "And you'll know all about it. It isn't as if they can sneak off and do it. You'll see it coming."

"A baby." Helena's voice had lost its shrillness and took on a gentle, musing quality. "Yes, I suppose they might."

"Of course they will." And Elias devoutly hoped she continued to sound that delighted whenever Cristina got around to telling her about the impending arrival. "Look, Mom, I've got a lot of work waiting for me…"

"Yes, of course," Helena said. "Not so much work these days, though? Now that Dad has hired that nice president girl to help you."

Nice president girl? Tallie? Whom his father had "hired" to *help* him?

Elias wondered, not for the first time, just exactly what his father told his mother about the business. He also wondered what Tallie would think of her job description. He grinned, looking forward to telling her.

"She works hard," he told his mother, because that was very very true.

"Good. So you will have time now. Yes?" Helena sounded as if she were rubbing her hands together in anticipation.

"Mom, I—"

"Yes," Helena answered her own question. "Now you will have time to find yourself a wife."

"I had a wife," Elias reminded her.

"Bah. She was never the wife for you, Elias," Helena said. She didn't say *I told you so* because she hadn't. But she'd always been concerned about his decision to marry Millicent, though all she had said was, "Are you sure she will make you happy, my son?".

What she should have asked, Elias thought, was, can you make *her* happy? Because obviously he had not.

Now he shut his eyes. "Don't start, Ma—"

"She hurt you, Elias. But you cannot hide away forever."

"I'm *not* hiding!"

"No, you are working. You are working every single hour of the day! And maybe that is not hiding precisely, but it does the trick."

He couldn't argue. She wouldn't listen. "I have to go."

But Helena, thwarted by her daughter, was not about to let Elias's disastrous first marriage destroy the possibility of a second one.

"I know the perfect woman. I was having my hair done last week. You know Sylvia Vrotsos who cuts my hair? She has a cousin who has a daughter—"

"Mom! Stop!"

"Beautiful girl. Sylvia had her picture there. You will love her. She's smart. Beautiful and smart. Sylvia says she is getting an MBA!"

Elias already knew a beautiful smart woman who had an MBA. He was sleeping with her.

"I will invite her to dinner on Sunday," Helena rattled on. "You can meet her then."

"I don't—"

"And if you don't like her, Sophia Yiannopolis has a daughter who is a stockbroker who just broke off her engagement to a lawyer from New Haven."

"Mom!"

But she was too caught up in her own ideas to even hear him. Thank God Rosie tapped on the door, then opened it and poked her head in.

"Someone to see you. Says it's important. How long?" she mouthed silently.

"Now," Elias mouthed back. "Mom, I have to go. I have a business to run."

"But the president girl—"

"Goodbye, Mom." He banged down the phone and glared at it. Then he looked up at Rosie. "Send him in."

She turned to the man in reception. "Mr. Antonides will see you now." Then she stepped aside and a lankier, scruffier Antonides strolled in.

"Hey, bro! How's it goin'?"

"Peter?"

His brother was wearing faded blue jeans with holes in the knees and a bright-red Hawaiian shirt with palm trees on it. His jaw was unshaven, his black hair windblown and in need of cutting.

"Don't look so surprised. I told you I wanted to talk to you. You never called me back." The voice was mildly accusing.

"I'm busy."

Peter looked around. "So I see." He held out his hand, and Elias shook it, still feeling a bit numb because "surprised" didn't quite cover it.

He hadn't seen his brother in, what, three years? Peter had gone to Hawaii for college ten years ago—as far away from home as he could get and still be in America, he'd told Elias. He'd been back perhaps half a dozen times since. On the rare occasions he had been home, stopping by to see Elias at work had never been high on his list of priorities.

He'd visited the Manhattan office once, about six years ago, and had hightailed it back to Hawaii the next day, confessing to Elias in a phone call weeks later that the mere sight of his brother neck deep in red ink and business ledgers while trying to sustain the family business had totally spooked him.

"I don't know how you do it," he'd said.

"Someone has to," Elias had replied sharply.

"Well, better you than me," Peter's tone had been fervent.

Elias had only seen him once since. A few Christmases ago on his way out of the city, Peter had stopped by his old flat on the Upper West Side to see if Elias could lend him some money— money that, so far, he hadn't paid back.

And he didn't need to think he was going to get more this

time! Elias had had it up to here with irresponsible relatives. He sat down again and gestured toward the chair on the other side of the desk. But Peter didn't sit down. He stared at the mural Martha had painted.

"Nice. She does good work." He didn't have to ask who had done it.

"Yes, she does." Elias straightened the papers on his desk, then picked up his pen and rolled it between his fingers, waiting for the other shoe to drop.

But Peter wasn't ready to drop it yet, apparently. He prowled around the office, juggled Elias's sea-glass paperweight, tapped his fingers on the doorjamb, then shoved his hands in his pockets. Elias watched him warily.

"Smart move coming over to Brooklyn," his brother said finally. "Hell of a good view of Manhattan."

"Yes," Elias agreed. "But I didn't come for the view."

"Obviously," Peter said, taking in Elias's windowless room. "It's all about finances, isn't it?"

"They are a consideration," Elias kept his voice even.

Peter nodded. "So how'd you like to be on the next big boom? Make a bundle. Sound good?"

Peter? Talking money? Talking about *making* money? Elias tried to bend his mind around that.

"Spell it out," he said at last.

"I've been working on a windsurfer."

*Working* on a windsurfer seemed, to Elias, an oxymoron. Windsurfers were play, no matter how much time you spent on them and how much money you went through while you were doing it instead of getting a real job.

But he held his tongue as Peter rambled on, talking about how he'd come up with this new idea while he was repairing an old one. His brother, in the throes of enthusiasm, had always been hard to follow. He waited, strangling his pen.

"Look," Peter said. "I'll show you what I mean." He went back out into the reception office and returned carrying a two-foot-square portfolio, which he proceeded to open on Elias's desk.

There were drawings, lots of them, surprisingly detailed and with lots of numbers and arrows and references to velocity and wind power, and Peter seemed intent on explaining it all to him—how it was a departure from current windsurfers, how it was faster and more maneuverable, and how it would be easy to manufacture and very appealing to the market. Peter covered all the bases, rambled on for half an hour at least. Then he stood back and looked down at Elias.

"So," he asked, "what do you think?"

Elias, who had actually been thinking about how he could get Tallie to come to his place tonight—maybe work late and offer to make her supper—blinked. "Think? About what?"

"About the windsurfer," Peter said with barely controlled impatience. "Didn't you hear anything I said?"

"Yes, of course." Well, sort of. Elias shrugged. "It's…interesting."

"So, do you want to do it?"

"Do what?" Surely Peter wasn't asking him to go windsurfing.

"Oh, for God's sake, Elias! I came all the way from Honolulu to show you the plans, to give you first shot—"

"First shot? At what? At building windsurfers?" Elias stared at him.

"Yes, damn it!" Peter snapped at him.

"Then, no, damn it, I don't."

It was Peter's bad luck to be the last straw. Elias was fed up with the lot of them—with his father, who only wanted to play golf, do lunch and sail; with his mother, who only wanted grandchildren and expected him to provide them; with Cristina, who was already irresponsibly providing a grandchild no one was supposed to know about yet; and now Peter, Mr. Surfer Dude, who only put in an appearance when he wanted something and now had some lame-brained idea for a windsurfer that would undoubtedly support his beach-bum lifestyle while draining money away from Antonides Marine!

Peter's jaw clenched, his eyes flashed. Then with barely controlled violence, he shuffled the papers back into a stack, slammed the portfolio shut and gripped it under his arm. "Thank you for your serious consideration," he said, sarcasm dripping.

"It's been so good to see you, so heartening to know you're as supportive as ever. Don't bother to see me out."

Everything in the room rattled when the door slammed behind him.

For a long moment Elias didn't move. He just sat there in the silence and wondered what the hell else could happen.

Would Martha show up to announce that she was running away with the gypsies? Would Lukas send a telegram from the back of the beyond saying that he was going to live out his life on a Himalayan mountainside and eat nothing but betel nuts.

There probably weren't betel nuts in the Himalayas, but when had logic ever governed anything the rest of the Antonides family wanted to do?

Elias stared at the door, waiting for disaster and wishing for Tallie to push it open and smile at him and make him whole again.

She didn't.

Because, he reminded himself, life wasn't like that. So he opened the folder on his desk and tried to concentrate.

He couldn't.

## CHAPTER TEN

"TALLIE? You're not listening!"

"Of course I'm listening, Dad." Well, sort of. Trying to at any rate. In fact, her brain was wrestling with a far more important issue—what had happened during last night's lovemaking with Elias.

"Then answer me, damn it. I got the report Elias sent. I'm concerned about the profits."

"Um…" Tallie fumbled with the papers on her desk.

Report? Elias had sent a report? Yes, she guessed he had. She had mentioned her father wanting one and obviously he'd sent one. Responsible Elias.

Irresponsible Tallie. Foolish Tallie. Blind, idiotic Tallie.

And none of those Tallies was in the least interested in talking business with her father this morning. She couldn't even think about it.

All she could think about was Elias—and that somehow she had fallen in love with him.

"The overall profits of Antonides Marine were flat last quarter, you know," Socrates went on.

It hadn't happened in a blinding flash the way it had with Brian. They had seen each other across the proverbial crowded room. They had walked toward each other as if destiny was pulling them together. They had smiled. They had spoken. They had felt an instant connection that had endured for the rest of Brian's life.

She had known she loved him from the moment she saw him.

Elias had sneaked up on her. Of course, he was handsome. Certainly he had a body to die for. He was smart, intense, dynamic, hardworking, determined. He cared about his family, his staff, even the interloper president who had come in and taken over what should have been his job.

The wonder wasn't that she loved him. The wonder was that it had taken her so long to realize it.

But knowing, she had no idea what to do.

Elias wasn't like Brian. He didn't wear his heart on his sleeve. On the contrary, he had it buried under more layers of steel-plated emotional armor than a Sherman tank.

And while Tallie was sure he genuinely liked her and certainly enjoyed going to bed with her, the word *love* had never escaped his lips.

"What's he doing about the profits, Tallie?"

"Profits?"

"Oh, for God's sake! Focus, girl. This is two quarters in a row that things have been a little flat. What's going on?"

Tallie mustered her brain cells. She forced her brain to backtrack through her father's words and pick out which things to respond to. "We're making adjustments. Streamlining in some areas, cutting back waste. And we're looking at other options."

"I know, I know. Some marine outfitter," Socrates said impatiently. "I damned well hope so because–"

"Because you have money invested." Which, besides marrying her off, was his other bottom line.

Marrying her off was what he'd tried to do by offering her this job in the first place! He'd *wanted* her to fall in love with Elias. He'd orchestrated the whole thing in hopes that she would get married and be a good Greek wife and stop trying to follow in his footsteps.

She wondered what he would say if she told him it had worked—the falling-in-love part, not the getting-married-and-being-a-good-Greek-wife part. Because if Elias hadn't mentioned *love,* he certainly hadn't mentioned marriage.

"You have some experience with this sort of thing, Thalia," he said. "You should be working with Antonides."

"I am."

"You are? Every day?"

"Of course."

"Then…what the hell's the matter with him? Doesn't he like women?"

*"What?"* Tallie's brain cells all got together on that!

"You heard me. You're not hard on the eyes, Thalia. You might not be a cover model—"

"Thank you very much," Tallie said drily.

"But—" Socrates steamrollered on, "you are clever and intelligent and you are under his nose from Monday through Friday. Why the hell hasn't he asked you out?"

*Because he didn't have to,* she wanted to say. *I fell into his bed without him doing a thing. And now we're having an affair and I love him and he's going to dump me and I owe it all to you.*

Instead she said, "Goodbye, Dad, and banged the phone down so hard the battery pack fell out.

She wished she felt the tiniest bit of satisfaction for having done it. In fact, she felt miserable. Elias wanted her in his bed, yes. But for how long? And when he got tired of her, then what?

Clearly she was not a woman cut out for affairs. She stabbed her pen through the papers on her desk and barely noticed. She couldn't work. She couldn't think. She stood up and stuck her crutches under her arms and hobbled out of the office.

"Rosie! I'm going to—" She stopped dead and stared at the back of a black-haired man in faded blue jeans and a loud Hawaiian shirt. "Elias?" She couldn't believe her eyes.

The man had been talking agitatedly to Rosie, but he turned at the sound of her voice and she saw, not surprisingly, that it wasn't Elias at all. He was wiry and leaner than Elias. Younger, too, and darkly tanned, but deeply handsome in the classic Antonides way.

"Thank God, no," he said, and clearly meant it. "I'm Peter. His brother. For my sins." His mouth twisted. But then he turned on his version of the Antonides charm and gave her a warm slow smile. "And you are?"

Tallie hobbled forward and held out a hand to him. "Tallie Savas. It's nice to meet you. What a surprise. You're the surfer dude?"

"Is that what he says?" Peter's smile vanished and sudden anger flashed in his eyes.

"No," Tallie hastened to assure him. "Elias didn't. Cristina did."

The smile returned at once. "You know Cristina? How is she?" he asked eagerly. "I haven't heard from her in ages."

"She's married."

Peter Antonides's jaw dropped. "Married? Crissie? I'll be damned. Who to? Where's she living? When'd this happen?"

"You should ask Elias. He was there."

Peter shook his head. "Big brother doesn't want to talk to me. I waste his time—and his money."

"Oh, I'm sure he didn't mean whatever he said to give you that impression," Tallie said.

"Oh, he damned well did mean it." Peter shoved a hand through his shaggy hair. "And right now I don't want to talk to him, either. I came all the way from Hawaii to make a proposal, to talk to him about this—" he slapped the portfolio under his arm "—and he blew me off."

"A proposal?" So it was business that had brought him here. "What is it?"

"A windsurfer. I designed a better windsurfer." Peter lifted his chin, as if daring her to make something of it.

"Did you?" Tallie's eyes widened. From what she'd heard from both Cristina and Elias, Peter was a surf bum, no more, no less.

But Peter was adamant. "Damned right I did. I ride 'em, but I've got a blinkin' master's in mechanical engineering. I know what I'm talking about. But Mr Fair and Square, Mr Good Business Head couldn't even listen!" He turned toward the door.

Instinctively Tallie caught his arm. "Elias has a lot on his mind right now."

"When doesn't he?"

"Possibly never," Tallie said quite truthfully. "But I'd be happy to listen."

"You?" Peter looked doubtful. "What are you? I don't mean to be disrespectful, but are you Elias's assistant or something?"

"Or something," Tallie said drily.

"Are you sure about this?" Peter persisted. "I don't want to get you in trouble. I know my brother. He's big on loyalty. And he can be a jerk."

"Elias and I have an understanding."

Peter looked speculative. Then his gaze narrowed as he assessed her more closely. "So, what do you do here?"

Tallie grinned. "I boss him around."

"You what?" Peter's eyes grew round.

"There's been a restructuring of the company. And I'm the new president of Antonides Marine."

"You? What happened to Dad? Good God!" The colour washed out of Peter's face. "Did he die and no one told me?"

"No," Tallie reassured him. "He just sold some of his share of the business to, um, my family. And we divided up the jobs." Which was the truth, of a sort. "And I'm president. I'm qualified," she assured him, in case he was wondering.

But he was grinning. "So what's Elias then? Chopped liver?" He looked as if that wouldn't have been a bad idea.

"Elias is still managing director. We work together." *We sleep together. We make love to each other.*

Except Elias didn't believe in love and— She couldn't go there. Not now.

"Come on." She herded Peter and his portfolio into her office. He looked sceptical, but finally allowed himself to be steered through the door. He looked around and whistled. "So you got the window. Heck of a view."

"Isn't it?" Tallie shut the door, then took a page out of Theo's book and rang Rosie's line. "Could you send someone down with coffee and *kolaches?*"

"*Kolaches?*" Peter stared at her in disbelief. "I guess there has been a restructuring. Elias would never have thought of that."

"A well-fed staff is a harder-working, happier staff," Tallie recited on cue.

"Well, maybe it was his idea, then," Peter muttered, getting annoyed again.

"Sit down." Tallie gestured to a leather armchair. "And tell me about this windsurfer idea of yours."

She didn't have any preconceived notions about Peter Antonides. He wasn't her beach-bum younger brother who had spent years in college while she worked and he surfed to his heart's content. So she had far more patience than Elias apparently had. And a good thing, too, as Peter, encouraged by her attention, drank coffee and ate *kolaches* and went on at length about this new windsurfer he'd designed.

He dragged out technical drawings and explained the aerodynamics and the wind-resistance issues and the best materials to use. He spoke with an urgency that belied the notion that he was a layabout. He was obviously enthused and excited about his project. And the more enthused and excited about it he got, the more he had a look about him very like the one Elias had had when he'd talked about the woodworking he'd done on his apartment.

It was a labor of love for Elias just as this windsurfer was for his brother. Listening to Peter, she wondered what Elias would be like now if he'd been able to follow his own dreams instead of having to take over the running of the family business. Would he be as enthusiastic as Peter seemed to be? Would he smile more and growl less?

"It's going to work. It *does* work," Peter was saying firmly, his dark eyes, so like his brother's, fixed on her own. "I've made countless prototypes myself. I've modified it, tinkered, tuned. And I've got it right. But I don't have the money to go into production. That's why I brought it here. I read in a business mag about some of the changes Elias has made, some of the new stuff AMI is doing. And I thought my windsurfer would fit in, that it might work out well for both me and Antonides Marine. Elias disagreed."

Tallie ran her tongue over her lips and thought about what to say. Elias had already said no. But he'd said no based on his emotions, not based on the potential value of Peter's windsurfer. She didn't know the first thing about windsurfing. So she certainly wasn't going to contradict Elias even though she thought Peter's explanations made sense—at least to her untutored ear.

She also thought that, on a gut level, it was a project more in line with Antonides Marine than Corbett's the marine outfitter was—*if* it was as viable as Peter thought it was.

"It looks interesting," she said at last, because it did. "Can I run it past someone?"

"Not Elias."

"No, not Elias. My brother. Theo's not a professional wind-surfer, but he knows a lot about wind. He races sailboats," she explained.

"Theo Savas? *Theo Savas* is your brother?" Peter looked almost awestruck. Then a grin dawned on his face. "Hell, yeah, you can ask him. That'd be fantastic."

"How about if you ask him yourself?"

"Me?" Peter was equal parts eagerness and apprehension. "He doesn't know me from Adam. I can't just burst in and—"

"You won't. I'll get hold of him and set it up. Do you have a number where I can reach you? He's out in Newport now. You'll probably have to catch up to him there."

"No problem. No one was clamoring for me to stay here." Peter flashed her another grin and rattled off his cell phone number. Then he gathered up his drawings, all energy now. "Just tell me when."

"I'll ring you as soon as I talk to him. But listen to me, Peter." She caught his arm. "I am not promising to overrule Elias's decision. I'm simply promising to ask Theo take a look at what you've got. If he thinks it's an idea worth exploring, then I'll talk to Elias about it."

Peter nodded seriously. "Understood. All I want is a fair shot. But if you guys don't do it, someone else will. It's going to work. And it will be good for both of us. I know it." He turned toward the door, then stopped and came back.

"Look," he said, "I know the burden has been on Elias for years. I appreciate that. I appreciate *him,* stubborn jackass that he is. But obviously, if you're here, someone has finally realized that he can't do it all. So thank God for that. All I'm saying is, I'm here now. And I'm just trying to do my part."

Tallie smiled and squeezed his arm. "I'll call my brother."

It had been, conservatively speaking, the day from hell.

First there had been his mother, ranting on about Cristina and missing her wedding—and hatching plots to set him up with a dozen available women.

Then had come Peter and his hare-brained scheme about the windsurfer, which was, Elias was certain, yet another way to extend his beachcomber life in Hawaii and not have to get a real job.

And then he'd tried to put together his notes for Tallie on the Corbett's acquisition, and his computer had crashed.

"You've got a virus," Paul said. He thought it might have come in on an e-mail from Lukas saying he was in Queenstown and he'd broken his arm skiing so if Elias had come up with someone who had a job for him, he hoped he could do it one-handed.

"I'll see if I can clean it up," Paul had disappeared with the processor, leaving Elias with no notes from the Corbett's meeting. So he'd told Rosie to tell Tallie to postpone it because Tallie had someone in her office.

Then his mother called back, having eliminated one of the women on her eligible brides list and added three more.

And Elias found himself shouting, "I don't want any of them!"

He wanted Tallie.

"No need to bellow, darling," his mother said, sounding a little wary now. "I just want what's best for you."

What was best for him was Tallie. She was always there at the back of his mind—her smile, her wit, her laugh, her touch.

He wanted her in ways he'd never even wanted Millicent. He could talk to her about work, about business, about woodworking even. She understood that. She would probably even understand the envy he felt when he'd gone out to see Nikos Costanides's boatyard. She understood him.

And he loved her.

In his ear his mother rabbited on, but Elias wasn't listening. He was waiting for the gut-level rejection of anything to do with love that he'd felt instinctively since Millicent had walked out.

But it didn't come.

Because Tallie was not Millicent.

Tallie was a whole different person. A genuine, loving, caring person. A kind, delightful, funny person. An enthusiastic, energetic person. Not to mention a passionate lover.

Who didn't love him.

That did cause his gut to clench. But he took a deep breath and let it out slowly.

"We'll find you someone, Elias," his mother was saying.

But he didn't want anyone but Tallie.

"Leave it to me."

Elias shuddered at the thought. "I'll talk to you later, Mom," he said. He needed to think.

But before he could even begin, Rosie buzzed him again. "Your father on line two."

He desperately wanted to have her tell the old man he wasn't in. But he knew his father. If Aeolus didn't get what he wanted, he persisted. Better to take the call now and think about what to do about Tallie when Aeolus was back on the golf course.

"Ah, Elias! How are things? I was surprised about your sister getting married." But not annoyed like his wife. Probably Aeolus was glad he missed it. He once said that if he couldn't wear a golf shirt or deck shoes, he never wanted to go. Now he asked questions about the wedding, said he was happy to have Mark in the family because he could always beat his new son-in-law at golf, and then he discussed the weather and his new nine iron.

As usual, Aeolus took his time to get to the point. Hurrying him along did no good at all. So Elias stared out the window and waited.

After the nine iron, they talked about a boat Aeolus had his eye on. They talked about Peter.

"He's in town?" Aeolus sounded surprised. "Haven't seen

him since your mother and I were in Honolulu in March. Haven't seen any of my children in a month of Sundays. Not even Martha. Dumped Julian and took off. You don't know where she went, do you, Elias?"

"No."

"Well, I expect she'll turn up in good time." His father dismissed Martha's absence with the same cavalier attitude with which he dismissed everything—except golf. "Played eighteen holes yesterday with Socrates. Beat him, too," he added with considerable satisfaction.

"I don't suppose you won the house back," Elias said.

"As a matter of fact, I did."

Elias sat up straight. "You're kidding."

"I'm not. But I must admit, I am surprised. I was joking when I said I'd like the house back if I won, and he agreed."

Elias didn't ask what he would have forfeited if he'd lost. He was sure he didn't want to know.

"He's worried about his daughter," Aeolus went on.

"Worried? About Tallie? What do you mean?" Elias was listening now.

"She's consumed by work. All business. Missing out on life. Her fiancé died a few years ago, and since then she's been on her own."

"Fiancé?" She hadn't mentioned any fiancé.

But apparently Socrates had.

"His name was Brian," Aeolus told him. "He was a Navy pilot. Tallie knew him in college. They were going to get married. But he was killed. Training exercise, I think. That's all I know."

But it explained a lot.

"Socrates says she's grieved long enough. She needs to get back out and meet people. Meet men."

She didn't need to meet any more men! She had one.

She had *him!*

"She'll be all right," he said firmly, and vowed it would be so.

"Easy to say. Not so easy when it's your child," Aeolus said. "Parents worry about their children. Like you. We worry about you."

"Dad—"

"You can't shut yourself off from life forever, Elias. You had a bad experience, yes. But you can't refuse to live."

"I'm *not* refusing to live!" How did this suddenly get to be about him?

"You have a bad marriage, you don't run and hide. It's like riding a horse," Aeolus rolled on. "You fall off, you've got to get right back on."

Elias doubted that his father had ever been on a horse in his life. "Who died and made you Roy Rogers?"

Aeolus laughed. "We care about you. You are our son. You work so hard for us. Every day of your life you give to us. It's time we give back."

"By finding me a woman?"

"It's for your own good, Elias."

"Don't do me any favors."

Aeolus sighed. "I'm not sure about these women your mother has found. But if you don't like any of 'em, I can find you a looker. I guarantee it."

"Thanks a lot," Elias said with deliberate sarcasm.

Aeolus was oblivious. "What are fathers for? I can fix you up with a chorus girl if you want. Just say the word."

The word Elias wanted to say wasn't fit for his father's ears. "I don't want a chorus girl, Dad."

There was a moment of disbelieving silence. Then, "You do *like* women, don't you, Eli?" His father sounded slightly aghast at the possibility that just occurred to him. "I mean, I never thought that was why Millicent—"

"Goodbye, Dad." Elias banged the phone down, then banged his head against his desk.

It was nearly six when Tallie finished writing up her final comments on the Corbett's matter. Then she read and signed the letters Rosie had left for her. She could have done them quickly and gone home, but she lingered, waiting, hoping that Elias would come in.

She had barely caught a glimpse of him all day. He'd had a computer crisis, Rosie had reported. He needed to reschedule his meeting with the Corbetts. Then he'd had phone calls, and his brother Peter, and more phone calls.

It was, basically, business as usual.

Her day had been busy, too, with phone calls and letters, reading reports that Paul gave her and finishing up her own on Corbett's. Then she'd spent time with Peter, had arranged a meeting for him with Theo and had rung him to tell him where and when to meet her brother in Newport.

But through it all, she had lived on the memory of Elias's lovemaking—the hunger, the passion and the promise of his last lingering kiss.

What promise?

She sat staring out the window, watching the sun set over Manhattan and not really seeing it at all. She saw Elias in her mind. She held Elias in her heart.

Where did they go from here?

A movement caused her to look around. And there he was, leaning against the doorjamb of her office, his top button open, his tie askew. She didn't know how long he'd been there, just looking at her. But the sight of him sent a surge of joy straight through her.

"Hey!" She smiled at him, but a smile wasn't enough. It broadened into a grin.

Elias straightened. "Hey yourself." He flashed her a quick grin, but as quickly as it came, it vanished. He cracked his knuckles.

"What's up?" Tallie said. He looked uneasy. She frowned. Had he heard about her talk with Peter. Was he about to jump down her throat and accuse her of going behind his back. She didn't want them to fight.

"I want to explain—" she began, but he cut her off.

"I've got a business proposition for you." He came into her office and stood in front of her desk. She thought he might sit down, but he didn't.

He didn't look at her, either. He cracked his knuckles again, then began to pace around the room, jamming his hands into the pockets of his khakis, then yanking them out again.

Tallie, watching him, felt her anxiety level rise. "What sort of business proposition?"

He stopped and turned to face her, meeting her gaze head-on, then took a breath. "Marry me."

Tallie had always heard that hearing was the last sense to go. But even though she could see Elias and, if she reached out, she knew she could touch him, her ears surely had garbled his words. She didn't know what he had really said. But she thought she'd heard the words *Marry me.* But, no. There was no way on earth he could have said that.

Could he?

All of a sudden her heart began to sing. Her fears vanished. Her earlier anguished, *I love him; he loves me not* evaporated.

She loved a man who loved her, too.

A smile began to dawn, but Elias didn't see it. He had turned to stare across the river at the Manhattan skyline. "I know you're not looking for marriage," he said flatly. "I know you don't love me."

"I—"

"But it doesn't matter. This isn't about love. It's just good common sense."

Tallie's heart caught in her throat. It *wasn't* about love?

"You ought to get married," he went on stubbornly, still not looking at her. "You should have a family. You shouldn't just have a job even if you love it. You should have more. A husband. Children. Your father wants you to have a family."

"My *father?* What does my father have to do with this?" Her voice was shrill. She knew it. She couldn't help it. Then she had a further horrifying thought. "He *told* you that?"

She would kill Socrates Savas. She would strangle him with her bare hands.

"No. Not me." Elias rubbed the back of his neck. "He told *my* father. My father told me."

And she would cut him up into little pieces, Tallie thought, mortified to the depths of her being. Thank God Elias had begun pacing again and wasn't even looking at her.

She took one breath and then another, then tried to sound rational when she was only feeling murderous. "And so you'd marry me," she managed to get out with some semblance of calm, "because my father thinks I need a husband?"

"Well, it would free you up to concentrate on business."

"You don't think I'm doing that now?"

"I think it's all you're doing. Well, not all." His gaze flicked to meet hers, and she saw color rise on his neck. She knew what he was remembering. She was remembering, too. But it had meant more to her, obviously, than it meant to him. "I just think it would make things run smoother. And you told me you wanted to focus on business the first day you were here. All I'm trying to do is make it possible."

She didn't answer. She couldn't have answered to save her life.

"I know about Brian," he said when she didn't speak. His voice was quiet, there was a hint of strain in it. But she didn't know what it meant. "I know you loved him," he pressed on. "That's fine. This has nothing to do with that. That was then. This is now. And I thought—I thought if we got married it would make things easier for you. Your father would stop mucking around in your life. You could have your career and, eventually, a family. And—" he shrugged awkwardly "—you have to admit, the sex is good."

Maybe her father wasn't the only one she would kill.

"The sex is good?" Tallie clasped her hands in her lap so she didn't wrap them around his throat—or any other vulnerable parts of his anatomy.

There was a hectic flush across Elias's cheekbones. "It is! You know it is. Better than good. It's fantastic."

"Yes."

"Well then?" He looked at her expectantly.

"Anything else?" she asked after a moment. "In this *business proposition?*"

Like *I love you,* for example.

Elias scowled. He raked his fingers through his hair, chewed his lip, paced some more.

*Come on, Elias,* she urged him silently. *You can do it. I know she hurt you, but I won't ever hurt you. I love you. You can say those three little words.*

"Fine," he muttered. "It would get my old man off my back, too."

She blinked, her mouth opening and closing like a fish.

"He and my mother are determined to do me a favor and set me up with every damn eligible woman in New York. My mother's got a list as long as my arm of women she thinks would be suitable brides."

"I see."

"No, you don't!" He was almost shouting now. "I don't want them shoving women down my throat. I can't think when they're plotting all these things. And now you're here, they think I've got time and I can spend all of it on these silly women and—"

"What a terrible trial."

"Well, it is. And you know it. It's the same thing your old man wants to do to you. So the way I figure it, marriage would be the smart thing for both of us. Then we can get on with the rest of our lives without them pestering us."

"And the sex is good." Tallie didn't know whether to laugh or cry.

"Exactly." Elias nodded emphatically, obviously relieved that she understood. "So how about it? Will you marry me?"

Tallie swallowed and prayed the tears wouldn't fall as she said the hardest word she'd ever had to say. "No."

# CHAPTER ELEVEN

As MUCH as she wanted to say yes, Tallie couldn't.

Marriage, in her mind, was a sacred covenant between two people who loved each other. It was a lifetime commitment that promised faith and love and trust and forever.

It was never just "business."

So all she could do was knot her fingers in her lap and shake her head. "No," she said again, hoarsely. "Thank you, but it wouldn't work."

She couldn't marry him for the wrong reasons. She couldn't love him when he only wanted "good sex" and easy business relations. But she couldn't explain. Not without looking like a fool. Not without admitting she had fallen in love with him—and wished he also loved her.

She chewed her lip and wished the earth would swallow her up, anything to get her out of this office where Elias stood staring at her as if she'd lost her mind.

But then he shrugged casually, almost indifferently.

"Whatever," he said lightly. "Just a thought." As if it didn't matter in the least.

Which should have made her glad she'd refused, Tallie reminded herself. And she would—someday. Really she would. But right now she just wished he would leave.

"So," he said after a moment. "I'll be off then." He started toward the door, then stopped and glanced back. "Afraid I'm not going to have time for any great sex tonight. I've got another commitment."

She felt as if he'd slapped her.

Tallie sucked in a sharp breath and could only nod. Determined not to let him see how much his flippancy hurt, she managed one word. "Whatever."

It actually physically hurt her throat when she said it.

For a long moment they just looked at each other. Elias's expression was stony, nothing at all like the man who had made love to her last night. Then, in what seemed like slow motion, he shrugged, turned and walked out.

Moments later the main office door shut. Not with a bang. Not with any emotion at all. Just a loud click.

In the silence of the empty office, Tallie sat for a long time after Elias left. Everything in her hurt. She felt gutted. As hollow and agonized as when she'd come home from Brian's funeral and realized that her life was stretching out in front of her—vast and empty and alone.

It hurt.

She hurt.

It was better, she thought, swiping away a tear, all those years when she hadn't felt anything at all. Then slowly, like an old woman, she stood up and hobbled out of her office and down the hall into the reception area. She stood by Rosie's desk and turned slowly, taking it all in—the break room where only crumbs and a dab of poppy seed remained of this morning's *kolaches,* the conference room where she had sat and listened to Paul and Dyson and Elias discuss and question and debate, where she herself had offered insights and had learned more than she'd ever thought possible, Elias's tiny office with its wonderful mural, the small library with its volumes of maritime history and shipping manuals and, most of all, its beautifully crafted bookcases that she knew now had been Elias's contribution.

The whole place—the whole business—was all really due to Elias's hard work. The rest of them added bits and pieces, but the company was his. It had started out as his family's, but he was the one who kept it alive, made it thrive.

She'd jumped at the opportunity to take the job when her father had offered it. But she hadn't deserved it. She'd done nothing to earn it. And even though she knew she had made a contribution to the business, she hadn't given anywhere close to what Elias had given to Antonides Marine.

It didn't matter that she was president and he was managing director, in the end it was Elias's company.

And it wasn't big enough for both of them. Not now.

She couldn't work with him every day—couldn't see him across the table in meetings or stand in the office and talk about day-to-day business matters and not ache for wanting him.

And she couldn't just settle for a hollow marriage and good sex. It had nothing to do with grieving for Brian. It had everything to do with wanting it all with the man she now loved. If she couldn't have that, she didn't want any of it.

She rubbed her hand over the smooth oak of the bookcase, and then she sat down at Rosie's desk and wrote Elias a note.

When she finished it, she put it on his desk. Beside it, she left her report detailing the reasons she thought they should pass on the Corbett's acquisition. She said her brother Theo would possibly be contacting him about a better idea. She hoped she hadn't overstepped her bounds.

At the end she wrote, "Everything I've done, I've tried to do for the good of the company. And that is why I quit."

She'd quit.

Elias sat at his desk and stared at the letter in his hand.

He'd found it on his desk just minutes ago when he'd come downstairs. It was brief and professional and to the point. Very polite. Very Tallie.

Very gone.

He sat there, staring at the note that trembled in his fingers, and he felt his throat close and his eyes burn. He clenched his jaw and tried not to feel anything. But he felt shattered. Lost. Empty. And furious.

Damn it all, anyway! How could she just walk out? How irresponsible was that?

Well, the hell with her. If that was the way she felt, it was better that she leave. He didn't need her.

But God, it hurt.

Not that he let on. He made the announcement at a hastily called staff meeting. "Ms Savas has left the company." He paused and looked at the shocked faces in the room. Then he added, "There are some bagels in the break room. Help yourselves."

They looked at him. They looked at each other.

"What happened?" Rosie asked. "Why isn't she here?"

"She just quit? For no reason?" Dyson's brow was furrowed. "I thought she liked us."

"I imagine she got a better offer," Elias lied. If she hadn't already, no doubt she soon would.

"Still seems odd," Paul mused, scratching his head. "Do you think we upset her?"

"No, I don't think you upset her!" Elias's tone was so sharp they all looked at him and blinked. Irritated at showing emotion, he shoved a hand through his hair, then took a steadying breath. "Just forget it, all right?"

He tried to forget, too.

He threw himself into his work. Over the next week he called Corbett and told him they had decided against purchasing his marine outfitter.

"We've decided to move in a different direction," he explained.

"But—" Corbett sounded stunned.

"We had long discussions about the future of the company," Elias told him. "It wasn't a decision made lightly. But while we're developing new avenues, we just felt that we should stick closer to what we know—which is boats—not clothes."

"It's that woman," Corbett muttered. "She didn't like us."

"Ms Savas is no longer with the company," Elias said. "In the end the decision was mine."

But it was true that Tallie's input had counted. She'd been right in her assessment, not of Corbett's worth, but of its worth to Antonides Marine. She understood AMI's focus. She knew its history, its successes, its failures. She had been a good president as long as she'd lasted.

She'd been a good friend. A good lover.

He tried not to remember. He worked day and night. He put up bookcases. He built shelves and cabinets and cupboards. He finished the first floor and went into the basement and knocked down walls.

He was tempted once to knock down Martin who asked what he'd done with Tallie.

"I haven't done anything with her!" he snapped.

Martin shrugged. "Then *to* her."

"Or *to* her!" Elias's fists clenched. His gut twisted.

He expected any day to hear from his father that she had got some other hotshot job in a bigger company. But his father said nothing.

Even when Elias asked point-blank if she was working for Socrates now, he just shrugged.

"Socrates hasn't mentioned her recently," Aeolus said. "I think he was shocked when she left without telling him. He doesn't know where she is."

No one seemed to know where she was.

Not that Elias looked very hard. But he couldn't help paying attention to what he heard. The trouble was, he didn't hear anything at all.

Tallie might as well have dropped off the face of the earth.

And then one afternoon about two and a half weeks after she left, he got a call from her brother Theo.

"That windsurfer works."

"I beg your pardon?" Elias didn't know what he was talking about.

"Tallie sent your brother out to show me the plans for his windsurfer. It's impressive. You should consider it."

It wasn't the windsurfer or his brother that caught Elias's attention. "Tallie sent him?" he demanded. "When?"

"Couple of weeks ago now. Maybe three." Theo couldn't remember. "I had work to do here. Pete came with me. We sailed up to Boothbay and back. Then we built his windsurfer."

"You built—"

"Yep. Tested it out. Very cool. Like I said, it's worth looking at. If you're expanding, you'll want to talk to him."

"I— Where's Tallie?"

"No clue."

"But—?"

"But I talked to her a couple of days ago. She said when I talked to you to tell you she was sorry."

Elias's heart stopped. "Sorry? About what?"

"Dunno. Quitting, I guess. Women are crazy. Even Tallie, and she's saner than most. Whatever the hell you asked her to do, you must have pissed her off. She just said if you'd asked for the right reasons, she'd have said yes."

She would have said yes?

Yes, she would marry him?

Then why the hell hadn't she?

Elias had wanted her to say yes. Dear God, he had wanted her to say yes!

And what were the right reasons? Well, he knew the answer to that. For himself at least, the right reasons to marry were for love and commitment and a lifetime together.

All the things he hadn't been able to bring himself to say.

He had said them once to Millicent, and she'd thrown them back in his face.

But Tallie wasn't Millicent.

Tallie was as pure and honest and forthright as the day was long. She told the truth. He was the one who'd been afraid.

He bolted out of his office, practically knocking down Rosie. "I'm out," he said. "I don't know when I'll be back."

He broke a speed record getting over to her apartment. He ran up the stairs because the elevator took too long. He hammered on her door and waited and waited and waited, desperate to say his piece.

And then the door opened and all the words he wanted to say dried up. His jaw dropped.

*"Peter?"*

His brother, wearing nothing but a pair of boxers and some shaving cream, grinned broadly. "Hey, Eli. Fancy meeting you here."

"Where's Tallie?" Elias pushed past his brother into the apartment, looking around wildly.

"She's gone," Peter said unhelpfully.

"What do you mean, gone? Gone where? Theo said he talked to her. When's she coming back?"

"Gone means not here. Not sure where she went. Not sure she knew. Gone walkabout, I think Lukas would say."

"That's ridiculous! She wouldn't do anything of the sort. What are you doing here? And why are you…undressed?"

"Because I just took a shower. And now I'm shaving," Peter said, "because I have a hot date tonight, and I want to impress the lady in question with my smooth skin. And I'm here because I'm living here."

Elias gaped. *"What?"*

Peter shrugged. "As much as I would love to make you think I'm living with Tallie, because I know it would annoy the hell out of you, the truth is I'm cat-sitting."

Elias stared in disbelief.

At that moment, as if on cue, Harvey wandered out of the bedroom, meowing. "Cat-sitting," he echoed. "So she…really isn't here."

"Read my lips," Peter said wearily. "She really isn't here."

"And she hired you to cat-sit? For how long?"

Peter shrugged. "However. She didn't say. She just offered me her place for the time being—while I find a manufacturer for my windsurfer."

The windsurfer he'd tried to interest Elias in. The windsurfer Elias had flat-out rejected because he couldn't believe that Peter was doing any more than wasting time. But Tallie had believed. At least enough to send him to her brother.

That was what her reference to Theo in her note had been

about. It made sense now. One more thing she'd done for the good of the company.

"Let me see it again," he said gruffly.

"Don't do me any favors." Peter's reply was equally brusque.

"I'm not doing you favors, damn it," Elias snapped. "I'm doing business. If it's a good product—and Tallie and Theo apparently think it is—then we might well be interested."

Peter's dark brows lifted. "You're serious?"

"Yes. Bring it by the office tomorrow." Elias paused. "Tell me where she is."

"I don't know. Honest. She called me a couple of days ago. She was in a hurry, she said. Had someplace to go pronto. Wanted to know if I was planning to stick around the city, wondered if I'd be interested in living in her place. I said I'd be more interested if she was here." Peter grinned.

Elias ignored that. "And she didn't say where she had to go?"

"No idea. But I gather she's going to be gone a while. She said if I needed to leave before she got back to take Harvey out to her folks' house."

"I have to find her," he said simply.

Peter gave him a not unsympathetic smile. "Good luck, bro."

It shouldn't have been hard.

A woman with Tallie's talents and business reputation should have been easy to track down. This was the information age, after all. If you knew their habits, discovering anyone's whereabouts was a piece of cake.

Sometimes.

Not this time.

Elias tried asking his father again if Socrates had said anything about Tallie—where she was, how she was doing, if she liked her new job.

Aeolus shook his head. "She called him a few days ago. He offered her a job as his vice president in charge of Pacific Northwest operations. Can you believe she turned it down?"

Elias couldn't. Not at first. He knew she'd always wanted to work for her father. But maybe she didn't want him trying to shove more potential husbands down her throat. With her résumé she could take her pick of job offers.

He'd just have to use a corporate headhunter to track her down.

The headhunter struck out. "I have a lot of people I could send to you for interviews if you want a new president," he told Elias.

But Elias didn't want anyone else. He only wanted Tallie.

So he set about trying to find her himself. He spent a good chunk of every day trying to track down Tallie Savas. He spent more time trying to find Tallie than he did working for Antonides Marine.

To his surprise, Peter took up the slack.

His brother came in with his plans for the windsurfer, stayed for a meeting and after that showed up every morning at eight.

"What?" Peter challenged when Elias looked astonished. "You don't think I can handle this?"

"Just surprised," Elias said. The world seemed full of surprises.

But the biggest one—and the most painful one—was that days went by, weeks went by, and he never found Tallie anywhere.

Helena, who had heard through Peter and Cristina that Elias was consumed with a search for Tallie Savas was delighted. "I knew you would want a nice Greek girl," she said happily. "I can find you a nice Greek girl, Elias."

But Elias was done with subterfuge. "I don't want any other nice Greek girl," he told his mother. "I want Tallie. I love Tallie."

He told everyone else because he couldn't tell her.

Sometimes, it felt as if he'd dreamed the whole thing, as if she wasn't really real. But other people remembered her, talked about her, wished that she was there to tell about a grandchild's piano recital or a baby's first tooth, or to bring in some of her *linzertorte* or *apfelstrudel*.

Even that self-absorbed pompous ass Martin remembered Tallie's *apfelstrudel*.

Elias had brought in some from the local bakery that morning and he had the misfortune to ride up in the elevator with Martin who sniffed appreciatively, then said, "Probably not as good as Tallie's."

"No." He and Martin could agree on that.

"She is a fantastic cook," Martin said. "But it's a bloody waste of talent, her apprenticing herself to a Viennese baker, for God's sake."

Elias, who had been tapping his toe and ready to bolt the moment the door slid open, stopped dead. "What?" he said quietly. "She did *what?*"

With Martin he stood every chance of getting a lecture on the guild system and why apprenticeships were going to be ringing the death knell of Central European crafts—or whatever. And he did. But eventually he also got, "She's got some daft notion of becoming a baker."

"A baker?" Elias stared at him. "Tallie? Where?"

Martin rolled his eyes. "Viennese bakers are generally in Vienna."

"Tallie's in Vienna? How do you know?"

Martin shrugged. "I ran into her last week when I was there doing a story on the UNO."

Her workday started at 4:00 a.m. Tallie was there even before Heinrich, the master baker. She did all the low, tedious jobs that fell to the newest apprentices. Heinrich was a Viennese version of Socrates Savas—and Tallie was having to work her way up.

She cleaned and scoured and scrubbed and then she measured and ground and kneaded and rolled. She worked long, hard hours in the kitchen in the morning and in the shop in the afternoon.

It was a far cry from the fast track of corporate America, but the truth was that she was doing something she loved. It had been her hobby, her stress-reliever, and ultimately it had been her salvation.

She was happy. She was challenged. She was learning German. And she could actually go an hour or two at a time without aching for the loss of Elias.

Of course, she reminded herself as she filled the display cases before the afternoon onslaught of schoolchildren, she'd never really had Elias. They'd had "great sex." The rest had been all in her mind.

The door opened and Frau Steinmetz came in. A regular, she always ordered the same thing. Now she said, "*Grûsse Gott. Zwei strudel, bitte,*" and let Tallie practice her German on her.

Tallie filled her order, took the money, then counted out the change. Frau Steinmetz listened, nodded, corrected her pronunciation, told her that her German was getting better and so was her baking.

The door rattled again and, as Frau Steinmetz said, "*Bitte,*" and departed, two more women came in. Tallie waited on them, then on a group of schoolboys who banged in and milled around.

They were always a challenge, the orders coming thick and fast.

"*Pfeffernusse, bitte,*" a little boy pointed.

"*Funf powidlkolatschen,*" said a bigger one.

"*Vanillekipferln, bitte,*" said a third.

Tallie took all the orders, made all the change, laughed and chatted with them, then looked up to watch them dash out the door with their purchases—and saw Elias standing there.

For a moment she couldn't believe her eyes. She had dreamed of him so often, had let her mind drift over memories of his strong handsome face, his hard jaw, his lean muscular body, his lopsided grin.

Her memories paled against the real man.

Her knees wobbled. Her stomach lurched. She swallowed against a sudden hard lump in her throat. Instinctively she reached for the counter and hung on. He wasn't grinning.

He was looking at her as intently as she was looking at him.

"Elias?" What was he doing here? How had he found her? *Why* had he found her? Or was it just happenstance, one of those odd coincidences like the way she'd run into Martin in the Stephansplatz last week.

Elias closed the door behind him. "Tallie."

She wanted to run to him, to throw her arms around him, to hang on and never let go. But she couldn't. Not when she didn't know why he was here.

"Can I help you?" she asked in English.

His lips quirked. "I don't know. I hope so. I need to show the woman I want to marry that I love her. Any suggestions?"

She couldn't even breathe now. "You...love?"

He nodded. "Always have. Just too stupid to say so. Too afraid," he corrected, meeting her gaze honestly. "After Millicent, I thought I could protect myself if I didn't admit it. I was wrong."

"I'm not Millicent!"

He smiled slightly. "No, thank God. You're not at all like Millicent. You are honest and brave and forthright and gorgeous and—"

Tallie's heart was singing. She almost laughed. "Thrifty, strong and reverent?" she said. "Like a regular Boy Scout."

"Believe me, if you were a Boy Scout, I wouldn't be asking you to marry me," Elias grinned. Then the grin vanished and his expression grew grave. "Will you marry me, Tallie? For the right reasons this time? For love and honor and commitment. Forever?"

"Yes. Oh, Elias, yes!" And then Tallie did her best to fling herself into his arms.

It wasn't easy kissing a man over the top of a bakery counter. There was a lot of cabinet in the way, for one thing. There was a stern Viennese baker lecturing them in fast and furious German for another.

"What's he saying?" Elias wanted to know. He was still kissing her and she was kissing him. It had been so long. She couldn't get enough of him.

"He wants to know if you're buying anything. If not, he wants you to move along," Tallie reported with a grin.

"Ask him how much he wants for the woman behind the counter?"

"She's yours. For your love, you've got her forever," Tallie promised.

Elias hauled her right over the counter and wrapped his arms around her and kissed her with all the love he had in him. "It's a deal."

* * *

Her flat was about the size of Harvey's litter pan. It was on the top floor of an apartment block that looked like something out of *Stalag 17*. But it had a bed, and they fell into it the minute they got there.

Buttons popped, zippers slid. And then they were skin to skin, heart to heart. And for all that Elias wanted to take it slow and show her how much he loved her, Tallie didn't let him.

"We can go slow later," she told him. "We've got forever." She looked him in the eyes. "Don't we?"

"We do," Elias vowed. He kissed her, rocked her, then slid inside her and knew how much more it was than great sex.

"I love you, Tallie Savas," he whispered later. "Don't ever leave me again."

"Never," Tallie promised. She kissed him long and slow and deep. "I didn't want to leave you in the first place. But I couldn't—couldn't marry for less than love."

"Neither could I," Elias said. "I just couldn't admit it." He stroked a hand down her smooth skin, loving the feel of her, wanting her again, even though he'd just had her, but happy to wait, too, because they really did have time—and each other.

"Are you serious about baking?" he asked. "Really?"

"I am. I thought I wanted all the business stuff—and it is exhilarating—but the baking centres me. Like your woodworking," she added, giving him a sideways glance, expecting him to dispute it as he had last time. But he didn't.

"I was thinking about that on the flight over," he said. "Thinking about Pete's windsurfer and Nikos Costanides's boatyard and envying them just a little."

"You saw Peter's windsurfer?"

He nodded. "We're doing it. Theo recommended it. He said you thought it was worth looking at."

"I was leaving it up to you. I just thought maybe—"

"You were right. You were right about Corbett's, too. We didn't buy it. We're doing Pete's windsurfer instead. And he's come onboard as a vice president."

"Peter?"

"Will wonders never cease?" Elias said drily. "He's actually gung-ho about the business now. So I was thinking I might…try my hand at a boat or two. Building, I mean." He seemed almost tentative.

Tallie beamed. "Really? Like Nikos?"

"If you don't mind. Someday I'd like to have what he's got."

"I want you to do what makes you happy," Tallie assured him.

"Boats, then," he decided. "And working with Pete. But mostly—" he looked deep into her eyes "—loving you makes me happy."

"Likewise," Tallie said, nestling against him, laying her head on his chest, listening to the sound of his heart, loving it. Loving him.

Then she lifted her head and looked down at him, still smiling. "We could get to work on it now, you know," she said. "What Nikos has got."

"You want to build a boat?"

"No, darling." Tallie kissed his nose, his chin and then let her lips linger on his lips. "I want to get started on the three stair-stepsons!"

HARLEQUIN *Presents~*

# MODELS & MILLIONAIRES

### Escape to a world of absolute wealth, glamour and romance...

In this brand-new duet from Julia James, models find themselves surrounded by beauty and sophistication. It can be a false world, but fortunately there are strong alpha millionaires waiting in the wings to claim them!

### On sale this May,

Markos Makarios thinks Vanessa is the best mistress he has ever had—until he has to warn her not to think of marriage. Mistresses are only for pleasure, after all....

# FOR PLEASURE... OR MARRIAGE?
## by Julia James

*Get your copy today!*

HPMM0506